THE DROW HUNTER

THE DROW HUNTER

ALISON BROWNSTONE™ BOOK EIGHT

JUDITH BERENS   MARTHA CARR   MICHAEL ANDERLE

DISRUPTIVE IMAGINATION®

THE DROW HUNTER TEAM

Thanks to the JIT Readers

Nicole Emens
Diane L. Smith
Jeff Eaton
John Ashmore
Daniel Weigert
Misty Roa
Peter Manis
Paul Westman
Micky Cocker

If we've missed anyone, please let us know!

Editor
SkyHunter Editing Team

DEDICATIONS

From Martha

To everyone who still believes in magic
and all the possibilities that holds.
To all the readers who make this
entire ride so much fun.
And to my son, Louie and so many wonderful friends who
remind me all the time of what
really matters and how wonderful
life can be in any given moment.

From Michael

To Family, Friends and
Those Who Love
To Read.
May We All Enjoy Grace
To Live The Life We Are
Called.

CHAPTER ONE

Alison's phone rang as she stepped out of her car in the condo building's cavernous parking garage. The timing was perfect. She smiled as she glanced at the screen and saw the caller's name. Certain calls were always welcome.

It hasn't even been that long since we last talked, although I definitely won't complain.

"Hey, Mom." She closed the door of her Fiat behind her. "I don't have news yet about our new place. Mason and I are still looking. We've decided to take our time to find something that really works. He's been cool about that. Plus, I have to make sure Sonya's not crowded. I already feel bad about making her move when she has barely settled in."

"That's nice of you." Shay chuckled on the other end. "But I'm surprised you haven't stuck her with Tahir full-time. James might have brought you in, but you spent most of your time at the school for those first few years."

"Tahir's a great teacher, but he can be difficult sometimes, and the poor girl needs a break every now and again. I like him and he's talented, but I don't know how I would react if I was trained by him and had to spend every second with him. Even though I was at the School of Necessary Magic, I had my own dorm room with my friends and was far away from the professors' cottages. And when I trained with the Drow, they kept their distance except when we practiced magic."

"I suppose that in a way, this is another Brownstone family tradition."

"What is?"

"Taking in teens with shitty parents and giving them the support they need so they can have a chance at a halfway decent life." She snickered. "It's probably one of our less questionable traditions, as opposed to mass destruction and leaving heaps of bodies lying around when we are involved in something." Her light laughter died off. "That's not really what I called about, though. I have some…news. It's big news, too. Not bad, but…it has implications for all of us."

I should have known. It's been a little too long since I last heard anything, but maybe I'm overreacting.

"News?" Alison demanded, a little tense at this unexpected turn in the conversation. "What news? I didn't see anything about any explosions in LA, and if Dad was up to his old habits, it'd be hard to hide that." She winced. "Unless the government is covering up. Please tell me it wasn't that bad."

If the government was involved, it suggested certain unusual and dangerous enemies were also involved. They would most definitely be a concern, not only to the Brownstone family but potentially, the entire planet.

Shay's laughter returned. "No, nothing destructive or super-dangerous, unless you mean to my future sanity and sleep."

"Huh? What do you mean?"

"I'm pregnant," her mother declared with the blandness one might associate with the purchase of new socks.

Alison's breath caught as she processed what she had told her. The words weren't complicated or difficult to understand, but they were incredibly hard to believe. Almost impossible, in fact.

"You're what?" she asked, her disbelief evident in her tone. "It sounded like you said you're pregnant."

"I know we never had the formal birds and the bees talk, Alison, but I honestly thought you knew how that works by now." The joke was somewhat strained and didn't help at all. "You're not exactly a little kid."

She rolled her eyes. "Ha-ha, very funny, Mom. Great joke."

"I know it is." Shay sighed. "But the joke doesn't apply to the part where I'm pregnant. That's one hundred percent true fact."

The half-Drow leaned against her car, her phone clutched tightly in her hand. She blinked and tried to concentrate in an effort to regain control of her thoughts. Honestly, if Dorvu the dragon had flown into the parking garage to announce that he'd decided to join a ballet company as their prima ballerina, she would have been less surprised.

"But that's not possible," she murmured. "Because of

what…Dad is, and it's not exactly like you're newlyweds. You lived together for years before you married. If you could get pregnant, you would have years ago."

"I know." Shay exhaled a contented sigh. "Trust me, I really do know. And it's also not like it didn't surprise the hell out of me, but you know how your dad's little friend likes to tinker with him. We had a discussion about it, and Dad checked, and his friend confirmed it."

"Why would Whispy care if Dad had kids, especially after so many years?" Alison peered furtively around for any drone cameras to make sure she wasn't on some sort of prank show. She didn't sense magic, so no one was recording her reactions—a pity, really, because that would have been a far simpler explanation.

Her mother barked a laugh. "I'm not saying that Whispy cares if we have kids. From what James told me, it had something to do with fine-tuning his basic regeneration rate. This was a side-effect, apparently. He even offered to 'fix it' before complaining, to quote your dad, about 'tactical and strategic inefficiencies associated with slow gestation and a long maturation period of offspring.'"

At that, Alison laughed despite her shock. "Priorities, huh? Some things never change."

"Yep. So that's where we're at. You'll have a new brother or sister soon. Talk about a generation gap. You'll be closer to our age than your new sibling's age."

Woah. This is really happening. I can hardly believe it.

She took a few deep breaths before she allowed the warmth to seep into her. "You know what? I'm really excited. Way more excited than I would have ever imagined."

"Of course you're excited. You're not the one who has to be pregnant. Did you really want a sibling that badly? You barely mentioned it before."

Alison sighed. "I didn't think it was even a possibility before. When I started to care for you and Dad, it wasn't that long before I found out the truth about him, and it all seemed pointless."

"And before?"

"Yes. Kind of." She frowned as she considered this. "I asked my biological mother a few times why she didn't have any more kids, and she always avoided the subject. I couldn't tell lies by sight then, but I sensed there was a reason. Given everything that happened with my biological father, she must have known, on some level, that it would be a bad idea and he'd end up a traitorous asshole."

An old woman stepped into the parking lot and glared at her. She scowled and shook her head in older-generation disappointment as she made her way to her car.

"He was an asshole!" the half-Drow shouted after her. "He deserved to be called that. He was a douchebag piece of shit who was better off dead."

The woman rolled her eyes and muttered something about young people and their potty mouths.

"Is there a problem?" Shay asked. "I can wait if you need to kick some ass."

"No." Alison snorted with irritation and managed to resist flashing a rude gesture. "It's only someone coming in at the last second of a conversation and thinking they know what's going on."

She took a deep breath. It'd been years since her biological father had betrayed her biological mother to the

Harriken. Some wounds never healed, no matter how much magic was available.

After a moment's thought, she opened the door to her car and slipped in. With the convertible's top up, it'd be easier to talk privately in the vehicle than to head to the elevator and go all the way to her condo.

"How far along are you?" She watched in her rearview mirror as the old woman glared at her once more before she entered her car.

"Only a couple of weeks. I was curious—it was like I knew, so I decided to check."

"This is wild. Wait." Alison tensed. "Does Dad know?"

This could be bad.

"Yeah," Shay replied. "I told him before I told you. That's how I know about all of Whispy's modifications, remember? He had the same basic reaction. He seems happy but is definitely overwhelmed and surprised."

"I can understand that. It's been years. My guess is that he never thought he would have to worry about personally taking care of a little kid."

Her mother snorted. "If he can be a class-six bounty hunter and establish a barbecue empire, he can handle a kid."

The old woman finally pulled out, her expression still scrunched into one of disgust.

"I'm not saying he can't, only that it's a big surprise." Alison blew out a breath and refocused. "That's some crazy —" She sighed. "You can't help me. I just realized that. Not that the world revolves around me, of course."

"Huh? What are you talking about?"

She leaned forward, raised her free hand, and chanted

to summon a quick silence bubble around her. Most people already knew her father was different, even if they didn't realize how different, but the next turn in the conversation treaded on more dangerous ground.

"What was that, Alison?" Shay asked. "It sounded like a spell."

"Is the phone secure on your end?"

"One sec." Scratching followed for a brief moment. "It is now."

Alison swiped a few times to access an app Tahir had installed. "Okay, I wanted to be certain. We're close, Mom. Close to the dark wizards. It's not like it'll happen tomorrow, but it'll definitely go down in the next nine months. While I'm all for pregnant women staying active, I think helping to attack a group of murderous dark wizards goes well beyond the doctor's recommended daily exercise routine."

Shay sighed. "Obviously, I can't disagree with that. I hadn't really thought about it, but yeah, I have no idea what would happen to the baby if I was hurt and had to take a healing potion."

"I'm not mad. I want to be clear about that. Even with only my team, we can kick a lot of ass, and it won't only be us. I would have loved the help, but we'll be fine without it."

"That's for certain. I know you already talked to your Dad about helping, and he made it clear to me he won't sit on the sidelines, even if the government wants to make him do so. I don't think that will happen, anyway, but it's worth mentioning."

Alison shifted in her seat and adjusted her phone. "You don't?"

"Nope. The way he's worked it in the past is that as long as he stays one step down from that top level, they don't seem to mind. To be honest, it's not like he can pull that off without a lot of help, anyway. I think as far as the government is concerned, he's their little pocket nuke they can activate if necessary and throw at someone."

She released a dark chuckle. "But the point is that even without that, let's face it, your dad kicks a lot of ass. He might not be able to do everything you can do, but he can probably take more punishment and come back from it better than almost anyone on this planet. I'm tough, but I can't even pretend I'm as tough as him. He'll have to kick twice as much ass, though, to make up for my missing share."

"You might get lucky," she suggested. "Maybe this doesn't happen for a year, and you can come and cut down a bunch of bastards for me. Hana loves your old sword, but she'll gladly give it back to you. She's a Shay fangirl."

"I think I'll survive but I'm disappointed I won't be able to help you." Shay fell silent for a few seconds. "But do you really think it'll happen soon?"

The half-Drow glanced into the mirror and frowned at the bags under her eyes. Too much work and concern and not enough sleep, she acknowledged.

"Izzie's been in communication more," she explained, "and Tahir is digging deeper. We're much closer than we've ever been. When the time comes, we'll strike hard and fast, and that will be that. It's not like we have to kill every dark wizard in the world. We only need to end this Seventh Order. If their leaders are dead, I think it'll be over."

"I can't say it's a bad plan. It's not like anyone has really bothered your father or me in years. That said, I know that 'cut the head off the dragon and the rest dies' is good advice, but it doesn't hurt to cut the head and the tail off, and chop the body into little pieces, too."

Alison's instinctive laugh emerged more like a snort. "Once we find the place, I won't exactly go in there for tea and crumpets. Don't worry. I'll make you proud and make sure all my friends and family are safe."

"You always do, Alison. You always do. Okay, I have to go—oh, a little warning. I also passed on to your dad that you're gonna move in with Mason. He took it about as well as a five-year-old told he can't go to the candy store."

Alison groaned. "Really? Will he come up here and threaten Mason?"

"Nope. I've talked him out of it and I have him thinking about another one of his little barbecue road trips. I simply thought you should know. Okay, talk to you later for real this time. I love you."

"I love you, too, Mom."

The call ended, and she rolled her eyes. She wasn't sure which was more annoying—the Seventh Order or her father's overprotectiveness.

CHAPTER TWO

Izzie sipped her ginger ale, seated in a dark corner of the Liverpool pub. Raucous laughter resounded above the constant chatter of men and women packed together, drinking and enjoying life. The bounty hunter would have preferred a little alcohol, but this was one night she couldn't risk clouding her mind, not when she was on the job.

Across the bar, four men in suits sat in a booth sipping IPAs while they conversed cheerfully. No one else in the bar had reacted when they'd cast a spell after they'd seated themselves. She didn't know what spell it was offhand, but she suspected it was some kind of sound filter.

The men were wizards. Even if she hadn't tracked them for the past several days, she could tell simply by looking at them—one of the perks of being Izzie Berens. Even Alison didn't possess that handy little ability.

Thanks to Alison and Tahir's information, the bounty hunter had been able to find numerous new leads on the Seventh Order, which allowed her to better filter for targets. She had considered assassinating Conrad Barnes several times, but even though she was confident she could get through his security and body doubles, killing only one of the leaders of the group wouldn't be enough. Worse, it might even push the remaining few so deep underground that it would take years to find them.

There were four leaders. She knew that now. Four targets she needed to eliminate to gain her freedom and end the threat to her family. Tonight's dark wizards were nothing more than additional clues who would help her identify and locate the four treasures at the end of this painful quest that had dominated the last third of her life.

The men stood and nodded to one another. They glanced around and their gaze lingered on her for a few seconds before they made their way to the door.

Izzie hadn't used a disguise spell. Magic would have drawn their attention in the otherwise mundane bar. A simple disguise that included a blonde wig, glasses, and colored contacts was enough to fool them.

She rose from her seat and hurried out a side door. Once past the windows, she paused at the brick corner of the pub and murmured a stealth spell when she was certain that no one was watching her. The light around her bent and left a slight distortion that was hard to make out on the dimly-lit evening streets.

The wizards might sense the magic of the spell, but this wasn't a totally magic-free neighborhood, even if the bar was. Leaving a confined area and diffusing the magic around her would help prevent them from easily identifying her. She only needed to get close.

The four continued up the street, their low voices too

difficult to hear clearly at a distance. Izzie picked up the pace but didn't break into a jog or run. The faster she moved and the more noise she made, the more she risked the spell failing or a change in magic density. Either of those would draw the wizards' attention.

Small groups of people wandered the streets. One gaggle of cherry-faced men clad in red-and-white Liverpool FC jerseys wandered down the street singing a loud song about how much they appreciated the reign of King William and how it somehow improved the fortunes of their favorite team. Izzie didn't pay enough attention to sports to know how well Liverpool was doing.

"And God smiled on the reign of Old Queen Liz, and it's lack of intrigue," the men sang, "but we want to rule the Premier League."

Anger bubbled inside her as one of the wizards laughed at the drunken men across the street. The bastards were going to a pub and having a good time drinking while she and her family had to remain constantly on the alert for an attack that could come at any time. One of the reasons she had even avoided spending too much time around her mother and father was to provide a less tempting target.

Anything approaching a normal life had been denied her. Considering what her parents had been forced to do to her at the School of Necessary Magic, half her life had arguably been taken away because of dark wizards.

Rarely seeing her family had worked over the last few years. Dark wizards seemed far less inclined to even attempt to go after her mother, but Izzie wasn't sure if that was because they didn't think it was worth the risk of taking on Leira Berens and the Fixer without their daughter as a bonus or if they thought she would be an easier target by herself.

She had thought a lot about her life in recent months, especially after helping Alison in Seattle. Her friend's life represented what Izzie could have had, and she began to wonder if she should have spent less time hiding and more time daring the dark wizards to attack. The Brownstone clan had always gotten away with far more blatant challenges in their time. Maybe fortune really did favor the bold.

The main concern that held her back was the risk of collateral damage. The Mountain Strider incident was all the proof she needed that a dead student and a coma were minor compared to the level of destruction the Seventh Order was willing to tolerate—if not outright encourage—to achieve their goals.

Izzie refused to sacrifice innocent lives for her freedom. If she had to kill every Seventh Order dark wizard one by one until it was over, she would do it. But that didn't mean she wouldn't mind a short-cut to achieving her freedom.

If I get those four names, everything can change. We can end this. The order is already on the defensive, thanks to Alison.

A few minutes later, her quarry turned into a narrow alleyway. They had wandered away from the bars and pubs into a street filled with darkened and shuttered stores. There wasn't anyone else around except for the wizards.

Izzie narrowed her eyes and her heart rate kicked up. She cast a quick shield spell, no longer concerned that it would likely ruin her stealth.

A few more yards brought her into the alley.

Damn it.

The wizards stood in a rough V, their wands all poised. Their gazes darted nervously to search the shadows.

She resisted a snort when their faces twitched to evidence their unease.

"Whoever you are, you're in trouble," one of them stated. His fingers tightened around the shaft of his wand. "If you don't want to be seriously hurt, you'd better show yourself right damned now."

I'll need to do this quickly. There are too many places filled with people nearby.

Her smile turned feral. The men's magic remained concentrated around their wands. The fools probably thought she was an opportunistic magical mugger. Otherwise, they wouldn't have left themselves so open.

"We can see and sense enough of you," the wizard continued and gestured at her with his wand. "We'll give you until ten, and if you don't show yourself, you'll die."

Izzie murmured a quick spell while she made careful movements. The new magic disrupted her stealth spell to reveal the bright glow around her hands.

Her adversaries' eyes all widened.

"Berens!" one of them shouted.

"Too late." She thrust her hands forward to launch two bolts of light magic. They blasted into a wizard, who groaned and fell backward, the front of his chest burned. Using the distraction to her advantage, she ducked and ran forward.

An array of dark orbs and fireballs rocketed from the three remaining adversaries. They pelted her shield and stung briefly, but none made it through. She closed on another man and slapped her palm into his face. He grunted and lost his grasp on his wand as he fell back and his head cracked against the hard asphalt.

Izzie spun toward the two other men. She eliminated one with another blast of light magic. The arrogant fool might have survived if he had bothered to raise a shield.

The last wizard flipped his wand around so that it no longer pointed at her. She backed away, suspicious of the odd action and unsure of what his purpose might be.

He sneered. "Do you think we don't see right through you, Berens?"

"I think that whatever reason you want me is the same reason why you'll have trouble taking me." She raised her hands in front of her chest, her palms up. "Drop your wand and put your hands on your head if you want to live."

Her adversary gestured with his wand at the groaning survivor on the ground. "Like him?"

"He'll only have a headache. He'll live."

"No. He'll have a lot worse than a headache." The wizard shouted his spell. A fireball exploded from his wand and enveloped the wounded man.

Izzie blinked in disbelief. "What the hell? He was one of your team."

He sighed and pointed his wand at his head. "We'll all die at your hands anyway, Berens, if you have your way."

"It doesn't have to go down like this." She narrowed her eyes. "If you give me the information I want, I'll let you go. If I simply wanted to kill all of you, I could have done that at any time."

"We can't let you win," he replied, and anger flashed in his eyes. "We can't let you ruin what we've prepared for decades."

"I didn't start this fight," she shouted. "You bastards have targeted my family since I was in school. You can't complain that you're now losing a war you started."

The wizard laughed. "Losing? In war, armies lose soldiers all the time. You can't win a war without sacrifices. We're destined to rule this planet, and my family will benefit from my sacrifice."

Izzie lowered her hands with a heavy sigh. "Put the wand down. I only have a few questions for you, and you're probably already compartmentalized anyway. There's no reason to throw your life away."

"Do you know why you'll lose, Berens?" he scoffed. "Because you fight from the basest of motivations—for simple survival. We fight for something higher."

"Oh, give me a fucking break. Whatever weird scheme of world domination you have cooked up isn't some great spiritual quest, so excuse me if I don't fall to my knees in praise of your dark wizard glory." She snorted her disdain.

"We'll make a better world." The wizard closed his eyes and started an incantation.

"No, dro—" An explosion cut her protest off. She grimaced as her adversary's headless body sprawled almost at her feet.

Izzie frowned and shook her head. This wasn't the first time she had run into a fanatical Seventh Order dark wizard, but they had become increasingly more common in recent months.

There wasn't time to worry about it, though. It wouldn't be long before a police drone arrived. The battle, as short as it was, hadn't been quiet.

She slipped her leather gloves on and retrieved the

phone from the headless wizard's pants. It rang as she was about to slip it into her pocket. A moment of hesitation passed before she decided not to answer it. There was no way she would be able to fool whoever was on the other end. Instead, she hastened to collect the other devices.

All four buzzed with a text at the same time and she opened one to check it.

Don't worry, Little Berens. No police are coming anytime soon, but we will. You can run but you can't hide.

The phone grew warm, and she hurled it toward the far wall. It exploded in a shower of blue sparks a second later. She quickly lobbed the other phones into the alley and they all detonated before they hit the ground.

"Fucking Seventh Order," she muttered. "I need to end this."

Izzie covered the area with a quick illusion to hide the bodies from anyone outside the alley and pulled their wallets out to get their names and addresses. She wouldn't risk taking them as doing so would provide a focus for a tracking spell. Thus far, she had been fortunate that her anti-tracking ring, supplemented with warding, had helped to keep the Seventh Order at bay.

She scrawled the names and addresses on a receipt, tossed the wallets into a pile, and burned them with a quick blast of fire magic. Even handling them could potentially give her enemy a lead. If they held the cops away from the scene, the dark wizards would probably take care of the bodies themselves. She wasn't the only one who wanted to avoid attention.

With a last glance at the dead men, she jogged toward

the other end of the alley. She would have preferred to question the men, but at least she had names and addresses. Every clue gathered increased the chance that she would learn the vital information she needed to end the nightmare.

CHAPTER THREE

Hana hummed quietly as she strolled down the street. Her heels clicked against the sidewalk and she smiled at the paper bag filled with folded clothes—a few new dresses. She had considered a visit to a shoe store too, but she wasn't in the mood. The shoe fashionista muse was sleeping off a hangover or something.

The fox had tried to get Tahir interested in shopping with her on this trip—like she had every trip—but her boyfriend made it clear that he didn't understand her need to buy so many new outfits. Her massive wardrobe was one of the few points of ongoing contention in their otherwise contented relationship.

"You literally could change outfits every day and never repeat," he had pointed out during their last serious discussion of the matter.

"You say that as if it's a bad thing, babe. I want to be able to change outfits every day for a year and never repeat if that's how I feel," she had countered.

The infomancer was also disappointingly dubious about her plan to purchase a small warehouse for her clothes and somehow acquire a complicated magical artifact that would enable her to draw outfits from the warehouse directly to her apartment. She, on the other hand, considered it a goal to work toward.

Hana didn't care that her man didn't understand. She'd accepted a long time ago that the practically-oriented infomancer would never understand the joy that accompanied the ephemera of fashion. The very impermanence was the point and provided a layer of transitory beauty that filled her with even more confidence and happiness whenever she put on a new outfit.

And, of course, shopping with money she hadn't conned from some poor bastard was fun.

I wish Alison's sense of fashion wasn't so boring. Even if she's not as obsessed with practicality over everything like my babe, it all comes out a little too Little Miss James Brownstone. Even her mom is more fashionable than her. How does that work?

The fox frowned as she thought it over. Her friend and boss had technically been blind for most of her life until fairly recently. That probably had a lot to do with her lack of concern about what she looked like, even if the woman had been blessed with natural beauty.

A little laugh echoed her honest amusement at her own expense. She might be vain, but she refused to delude herself about the fact. There had been so much pain in her life that she would take whatever happiness she could find, wherever it might be.

She continued to navigate through the river of people that

flowed along the sidewalk. The scents of magic varied in the air and reminded her that even among the mostly human-looking crowd, she could never be sure who might be there.

I would know. I'm a woman who can turn into a fox.

Hana grinned and sniffed a few more times. She tried to imagine what it would be like to sense magic like Alison rather than smell it. Magic had never really smelled bad to her, so she hadn't wished for the half-Drow's ability. She wasn't sure if it was a simple lack of experience with the alternative that had somehow convinced her it was inferior.

A few Light Elves in designer dresses passed her. It was always interesting to see how some Oricerans had embraced Earth culture completely, whereas others dressed like they were extras from the old high-fantasy movies that used to be popular before the gates opened. Now, no one wanted to watch fake stories about elves and other magicals.

I wonder if that's why there are so many elf-themed cop shows now. I don't think I've ever personally seen a Light Elf cop. When there are so many of a particular race around, is it a big deal anymore?

Her thoughts drifted to Japan and Ryuji. In all the chaos of looking for Lily, it'd been easy to ignore her complicated feelings over her encounter with the other nine-tailed fox. Now that a couple of weeks had passed, though, they'd seeped back in occasionally to confuse her.

She honestly hadn't been seriously tempted by his offer to stay in Japan. Ryuji might have been attractive, but Tahir was hot too, and more to the point, she loved him. Still, the idea of not being the only one of her kind around held appeal.

Alison benefited from her Drow training, and maybe Hana could unlock hidden potential if there were more nine-tailed foxes around.

With a heavy sigh, she shook her head as she turned a corner.

What am I doing? I have a gorgeous and super-smart boyfriend who treats me well except for his anti-fashion evil. My boss is my best friend and totally awesome, and I live a stable life in which I can afford to go shopping all the time and don't have to con anyone who doesn't have it coming. It's fun, exciting, and sexy at times, all in one. I'm living the dream.

Something was missing, though. She couldn't deny that. There was something she couldn't put her finger on. The job provided more than enough excitement and money, Alison gave her rewarding friendship, and Tahir crowned it all with an abundance of love.

What is it?

Hana slowed and ran her tongue along the inside of her cheek. Her route down a side street toward where she'd parked took her away from the main foot traffic. Next time, she would be smart and park closer.

The uneasy thought of a hole that needed to be filled wouldn't subside. She tried to push it away by focusing on something else, but that only made it more prominent in her mind.

"Crap," she muttered. "I've been infected with Brownstone Brooding Disease. Thanks, Alison!" She shook a fist at the sky in defiance and earned a few curious looks from the pedestrians. "Why don't you pick up a sense of fashion from me in exchange?"

The fox continued down the street and shook her head. She tried to consider the possibilities that might explain her current issue. It wasn't that she wanted kids, that was for sure. She didn't hate them or anything, but she wasn't ready for the responsibility of a child, even if pregnancy would open up new fashion options. Sonya had been a nice set of child training wheels, enough to convince Hana that it would be many years before she was ready to handle a child. The last thing she wanted to do was screw over some poor little kid who looked to her for guidance.

Hmm. Do I want Tahir to ask to marry me? Not yet. I feel that if he does it in his time, it'll be better that way and that doesn't bother me. So what is it? It's driving me nuts.

Her frown deepened and she tapped the bottom of her lip. A different magical sword? No. She loved what she could do to their adversaries with the *tachi*. It was even freaking Japanese and made by Masamune. What more could she possibly ask or need from a weapon?

Did she need an awesome customized Brownstone Security motorcycle? Although she did like the idea of some ridiculously sparkly vehicle of doom and showing up like Seattle's sexiest superhero, she didn't even know how to ride a motorcycle. The aesthetics and colors she had in mind didn't seem like they would work well on a car either.

Huh. A few leather outfits might be in order so I can work out how I would look if I decided to go that route, but that's a project for the future.

Hana shook her head once again and shoved out the

thoughts of color blocking and tight leather. She tried to refocus on whatever it was that left her unsettled. Only the correct answer would free her.

A soft whine sounded nearby, and a quick glance to her side revealed a tiny brown puppy in a box in an alley. He wagged his tail and looked at her, his dark eyes pleading for her to pick him up and take him home.

Her heart melted.

"Oh…my…gosh. Literal puppy-dog eyes!" she squealed, gasped, and snapped her fingers. "That's it. That's what I'm missing." She pointed at the stray. "I'm missing you."

The puppy yapped once.

"Not technically you," she continued with a shrug. "But a pet. I begged Alison for one for a while, but I lived in her condo. She said no, and she didn't want anything other than fish for the building. Tahir's complained about the idea, but if I show up with such a cute puppy, what can he say? No? Ha—ultimatum time. If he wants his Hot Fox to continue to be his Hot Fox, he must allow for a cute puppy, and you'll quickly learn once you live with us that he doesn't care that much about a lot of stuff. He merely likes to complain."

Hana's nose wrinkled, and she sniffed the air. The acrid scent of rotted food drifted from a nearby dumpster, but that wasn't what interested her. An unknown but clearly magical scent seemed to emanate from the animal.

She set her bag down and walked toward the box, squatted in front of the dog, and sniffed. "That's not a spell, is it? It's you. Shifters don't smell like that, either, so…huh. This is rather mysterious."

The animal cocked his head.

"Huh. You don't look dirty or like you've been on the street for a while." She scratched him behind the ear and searched for a collar or tag. "But you have nothing to show who owns you, either." She frowned at the thought that someone had abandoned a puppy in a box in an alley.

He's so cute. How could you do that? Is this some evil billionaire thing?

"Of course, if you are magic, you might be an illegal breed or something that someone smuggled over or made with dangerous magical techniques." She tapped her lips in indecision. "But it's not like you chose to be made by some guy who didn't care or that you should have to suffer because of it. That's not fair, and if you are say…dangerous, what better person to look after you than someone who works for the Dark Princess? If you turn into a giant three-headed dog and start trying to eat the Space Needle, Alison can stop you, whereas animal control would end up dead."

Hana nodded, impressed at her impeccable and iron-clad logic. To leave the dog in the alleyway or call animal control would obviously represent a major threat to the safety of the city of Seattle. She had no choice but to take the cute little animal home and shower it with love and affection until such time as it turned into a dangerous killing machine. No, it wasn't even a matter of choice. It was her duty as a responsible citizen.

Her mind made up, she looped her bag of clothes over her arm and picked the box up. "Do you want to come with me? Bark once for yes."

The dog wagged his tail but didn't respond.

"I'll also accept that as 'I don't disagree with your plan, Hot Fox. Take me home and take pictures of me doing adorable things.'" She grinned and glanced over her shoulder to make sure no angry Kilomea was about to charge her and ask why she tried to steal his magic dog.

The happy dog barked the whole time that she all but skipped out of the alley and back to her car.

She was a magical fox. What could possibly go wrong?

CHAPTER FOUR

A dubious look dominated Tahir's face as he leaned back in his chair, his arms folded in stern disapproval. Hana grinned and stroked the puppy's head as she sat on her couch.

She had brought the animal inside and explained the circumstances of his discovery. Her boyfriend had listened quietly and intently, but his obvious irritation grew with each sentence in her somewhat convoluted and impassioned explanation.

"Let me be very clear about this," he began, his brow furrowed in grim determination. "You do realize that creature is magical, right? I know you smelled it because you said so, but sensing something and understanding and internalizing it are two different things. So, I'm asking you again."

"Yes, I know he's magical." She rolled her eyes and continued to scratch the animal absently. "And that creature? Jeeze, try not to sound so evil. Are you planning to collect a hundred more of him and turn him into a new magical coat?"

The infomancer straightened and confusion replaced the irritation. "What are you talking about? Why would I turn a dog into a coat?"

"Do you have a relative named Cruella de Vil? She's an expert on turning puppies into coats. Maybe you should ask her for some advice."

"Who is Cruella de Vil?" He looked more bewildered than ever and scowled for a moment. His mastery of Disney trivia obviously ranked nowhere compared to his extraordinary knowledge of hacking and various other esoteric subjects.

Sometimes, I feel so sorry for you.

Hana waved a hand dismissively. "It's a movie thing."

"You like movies where women turn dogs into coats?" He stared at her like he didn't know her at all.

"It's a cute movie." She shrugged. "But it sounds so twisted when you describe it that way. Never mind. Forget the movie and Cruella de Vil." She held the dog up. "The point is, how can you look into these adorable little eyes and question this little guy? He hasn't bitten me, didn't claw the leather seats in my car, and he hasn't tried to do anything destructive. This is the most chilled puppy in existence. I haven't even heard him so much as growl."

Tahir scoffed. "Attractive packages are often used to conceal deadly things. We both know there are many deadly beings, even those who aren't magical, who conceal negative behaviors for short periods of time."

"Like me?" She grinned. "I thought you liked mixtures of cute and deadly. Aren't they more interesting?"

Tahir scoffed. "Don't change the subject. My point is that it's not simply a dog that has an enchantment over it, like a tracking or healing spell. I would be able to tell." He shook his head, his lips tight with disapproval. "It's obviously some sort of inherently magical animal and considering that it's in the middle of a city and not untouched wilderness, and its painfully obvious attempts to pander to humans, it's unlikely that it's native to Earth." He unfolded his arms and softened his expression with obvious difficulty.

Don't pull a muscle there, babe.

"I want to be clear about this," he continued. "Many fauna native to Oriceran don't actually radiate magic like this animal. So this isn't simply some Oriceran transplant. That's what worries me so much. I don't like unknown variables. They make it harder to anticipate what the threat might be."

Hana laughed. "You're an infomancer-hacker. You crack systems all the time where you don't know what to expect."

"But I know the general range of danger I face." He shook his head. "But this dog could be a bomb for all I know."

"A bomb?"

"Yes, a bomb."

The fox beamed. "Then he's the cutest little bomb I've ever seen." She scratched him behind the ear, and he thumped his leg. "Aren't you, boy? Aren't you? A super-cute explosion who will kill us all."

Tahir frowned. "I'm serious. Even if it's unlikely to be a bomb, its magical nature makes it inherently questionable."

"So what?" She continued to pet the puppy. "Even if it's

not an Oriceran animal, many of those on Oriceran do have inherent magic. They aren't all dangerous killing machines that make the planet an awful place to live. Come on, babe. Being magical doesn't make something a dangerous threat, and if he was some wild killing monster, I think he would have already done something in the city and not waited until he ended up with only a few targets."

"That's true, but magic does increase the relative danger associated with it." He shook his head. "You have to understand that. You live it every day with the company. It's one of the reasons why your team typically carries out the magical assignments rather than Jerry's teams. The mere existence of magic increases the range of possibilities and the related danger, even when you think you're prepared for it. Magic is inherently disruptive."

Hana grimaced. "You're a wizard, but you sound like New Veil right now."

Is this for real, or is this only him really, really trying to talk me out of this adorable and special little guy right here? I can't tell.

Tahir sighed in exasperation. "Simply acknowledging a reality isn't the same as being a narrow-minded bigot or wanting all magic gone from Earth." He pointed at the animal. "I'm trying to explain to you that we don't know what it is, and the evidence points away from it being nothing more than a stray dog. It could be everything from a dog who happens to have magic to a dangerous creature sent from another dimension to wreak havoc on Earth."

"Not *it,* he." She laughed and the animal barked.

"That doesn't alter my fundamental point. I'm not engaging in pointless sophistry here. I'm simply trying to explain why I feel that dog presents a potential danger to you, especially since you seem so enamored of it."

"I like him because he's cute, and I've wanted a pet for months now. There's no deep conspiracy or mystery here, babe. Even you are susceptible to how things look." She gestured toward her body. "Fortunately for me and you."

Tahir gave her a flat look. "You're not a mystery animal, and your threat is known and quantified."

"Are you telling me that you think this puppy is some super-dangerous monster of doom that will destroy all of us if we let our guard down?"

He averted his eyes. "All I'm saying is that the possibility isn't zero."

"So far, he hasn't done anything dangerous or destructive," she observed once again. "He even barked to let me know he had to go, so he's already housebroken. Did you think about that? That's the obnoxious part of owning a puppy. We don't have to deal with dog poop, even using magic. I can take him to that dog park nearby for walks, and he'll have a great time. Better still, I'll finally have the pet I deserve as the Hot Fox, a Lead Investigator of Brownstone Security."

The infomancer drew in a deep breath and released it slowly, clearly in an attempt to stall to gather his thoughts. "It's housebroken. Of course."

"Yes. That's a good thing." She frowned. "But you look like it upsets you."

"It doesn't upset me, but don't you find that curious? Even a little?"

"What? That he's housetrained? What's so odd about

that? All it means is that whoever dumped him in that alley at least put some effort in."

"You don't understand what I mean." He shook his head. "It's curious that the dog is already housebroken despite being a young puppy. Perhaps it's not as young as I suspect, depending on the breed, but I know enough about features to believe that dog is very young."

Hana shrugged. "So he's a smart dog? Or maybe that's the point of the magic, and it would explain why nothing else flashy has happened."

Tahir arched an eyebrow. "Do you honestly think someone enchanted this dog or somehow bred him with magic to automatically be housebroken?"

Her breath caught, and she bobbed her head. "That's it. That makes perfect sense. He's probably part of some line exactly like that. Think of all the money you could make with a dog who doesn't need to be trained. Considering all the weird things and studies with magic out there, someone has obviously experimented with that kind of thing."

"I'll register my general disbelief in that as a possibility," Tahir responded. "Let alone as an explanation for this particular animal."

She grinned. "I'm only saying the possibility isn't zero," she taunted. "You can't prove me wrong."

"I also can't prove that you're not an ancient Kraken in the form of a woman. Don't use absurd logic."

"What's more absurd? Your theory that this little puppy is some dangerous beast, or mine that it's merely a cute little pet?"

He took another deep breath and shook his head, his

frustration building on his face. "Aren't you worried at all about a mysterious animal? What if it's a dark wizard trap? It might not be a coincidence that you're the one who found it."

Hana leaned over to nuzzle the dog affectionately. "If the dark wizards' schemes involve flooding the world with cute puppies who are already housebroken, sign me up for Team Seventh Order!"

A rapturous vision of a world overtaken by dangerous but adorable animals filled her mind. If the Seventh Order added a few cute teddy bear marauders to the mix, it would be perfect.

"I'm serious, Hana," Tahir admonished.

She rolled her eyes. "Are you really?" She straightened and fixed him with a more solemn look. "Come on, babe. I won't say it isn't a little strange, but you're an infomancer working for a half-Drow princess, and your girlfriend is a nine-tailed fox. A couple of weeks ago, that same girlfriend was in Japan helping said princess fight oni and tengu while onmyoji assassins were on our trail. We helped recover one of the three sacred artifacts of the Japanese Imperial Family, and we did all that while looking for a half-Gray Elf who can see into the future and spends most of her time as a tomb raider." She nodded at the dog. "But a cute puppy who is a little magical is a bridge too far into strange land for you? Come on. Who is the ridiculous one now?"

Tahir's mouth twitched, and he didn't respond. The seconds ticked by during which neither of them spoke. Even the puppy stared at the infomancer as if he waited expectantly for some incisive reason why the dog had to be transported to an ultramax or Trevilsom on Oriceran immediately.

"I'll check around," he declared finally and slumped as if defeated.

"Check around?" Hana responded. "Check around for what?"

He nodded. "It's like you told me when he came in. He's too clean to be a stray. There's no evidence that he's spent any significant amount of time on the street."

"Unless the magic is an always clean spell, too. Maybe it's a combination of useful enchantments bred into the dog."

"I doubt it works that way." He sighed again, still not convinced but at least a little more resigned. "But let's assume that's not the case. If he's trained, and it's not magic, and he's clean, and it's not magic, that means he belongs to someone. We have to perform our due diligence and look for the owner if only to save ourselves trouble if this is some valuable pet that has somehow been misplaced."

"You mean we have to look for the asshole who put him in the box in an alley?" Hana scoffed indignantly. "I'd like to introduce them to my other pet—my *tachi*."

"You don't know that anyone put the animal in a box in the alley. It might have crawled in. The point is that I think it behooves us to at least check to ensure no one is seeking the pet." Tahir pointed to the dog. "I already checked for subcutaneous chips or implants, and I couldn't find anything in the entire animal. I must admit, that makes me again question if this was someone's pet, but I'm willing to maintain the possibility at least."

Hana peered at her new and potentially temporary pet. "I suppose you're right. It wouldn't hurt to check a little, but if we find someone and they show up, I want to have a little discussion with them about how this tiny little dog ended up in an alley in the middle of a commercial district. I don't want him to end up in another alley somewhere else."

He shrugged. "Maybe they trained him to use a Currus —or they bred that into him using your logic."

"Very funny."

"Don't get too attached," the infomancer suggested. "I wouldn't pick a name for him until we're sure you won't have to immediately give him back to his owners. For a former con-woman, you don't have the best control of your emotions."

"No, being emotional made me a better con-woman. I understood people on a deep level. I felt their pain and joy." She smiled at the dog. "Besides, I can live with calling him 'the adorable puppy' for a few days. It's not an awful thing."

Her boyfriend stared gloomily at the animal, who barked once and wagged his tail. "Why do I have a feeling we'll regret this?"

CHAPTER FIVE

Alison eyed her friend as they settled at the conference table. Ava was in position and ready to take notes, but they still waited for Tahir and Mason to arrive. Hana had explained the situation with the dog on their way to the conference room.

"A magical dog?" the half-Drow asked. "And you're keeping it?"

The fox nodded. "He's adorable, and yes, I hope to keep him. Tahir hasn't found anyone yet who has tried to claim him. He didn't mention the magic stuff. That way, we can test anyone who shows up. If it is some special magical dog, they would have to know. That's what I think, at least."

Alison shook her head, open disbelief on her face. "This will end up worse than having triffles, but it's your home. If you can convince Tahir it's a good idea, you must have had some half-decent arguments. But if this ends with me having to collapse another bridge, I might have to make a few choice comments."

Hana grinned. "Sure, if that happens, you would have earned it."

Ava looked at them with a hint of a smile on her face but she didn't say anything. Her ability to all but disappear when in plain sight sometimes unnerved Alison, but she wouldn't be able to run her company without the English-woman's help.

If Ava ever decides to quit, I'm so screwed. I'll offer her ten times the salary if she tries.

Mason and Tahir filed into the room. They both headed to the seats beside their respective girlfriends.

Alison looked at the infomancer. "Did you have a chance to do what I asked? This meeting needs it."

He nodded. "Yes. Tell me when you want an explanation, and I'll oblige. It was…interesting, but I'll wait until you're ready."

Interesting? I suppose I should take it from the beginning before we explore the evidence.

She straightened. "Okay, I won't waste time because we have a job with a short fuse. It pays well—including an agreement to pay the full fees upfront—and they're very generous for something that will take basically a day."

"Upfront?" Mason frowned. "Not half?"

Alison shook her head. "The whole fee, but with an agreement to pay for any incidental expenses depending on what happens. It's very generous—the terms and the contract amount." She rattled off the total.

The others nodded. The offer was in line with a high-paying job that would take more than a day.

Ava tapped her tablet, taking notes, but made no effort to speak.

"But?" the life wizard asked. "You have your suspicious face on, and I don't think it's only because they'll pay up front."

"I have a suspicious face?" she asked.

"Definitely." He nodded firmly.

She chuckled. "There is a big 'but,' and yes, I was suspicious myself after the client offered to pay everything upfront. We've worked jobs before for desperate people who really want to lock us down by throwing money at us. It always requires extra caution to ensure they aren't desperate because they're wrapped up in something we don't want any part of. I've finally got the evil billionaires off my back, and I'm damned close to eliminating the dark wizards from my life and Izzie's. It'd be nice to be able to concentrate on nothing but the job."

Mason nodded. "So what's the catch then? What's the big 'but?'"

"It's a courier job," she explained. "In theory, it's simple. We transport a small box—that will be sealed magically—from Seattle to Portland. From what the client explained, she'll have a contact give us the box, but it'll be sealed in such a way that she'll know if it's been tampered with, and she doesn't want it opened."

"That doesn't sound so bad. I know we're not a courier company, but we have a reputation. I assume the big catch is that some nasty people want to lay their hands on it? That's not any different than many of the guard jobs we've taken. It simply means we'll guard a box instead of a person." He shrugged. "At least it won't get scared and run when we tell it to stay while we take care of the hitmen. I wouldn't mind a few more jobs like that."

"The problem is that the client is doing something I don't like. She refuses to identify what we'll be transporting." Alison frowned. "And she also insists it can't be transported through direct magical means, such as portals, which suggests it's something magically unstable and dangerous."

Hana shrugged. "Maybe that's why she's so worried about couriers and attacks. If she accidentally acquired an exploding artifact or something, she might be worried about how to get it out of the city without hurting anyone."

"Why not contact the government?" Mason countered.

"Because maybe she got it through less than legal means? If she's trying to avoid people being killed, I wouldn't hold it against her."

The half-Drow nodded but still looked uneasy. "I won't get too precious and frown at everyone who ever does anything illegal. Technically, half our jobs involve us violating computer laws, but I'm not all that comfortable with having no clue at all about what we might be carrying." She looked at Tahir. "I asked him to check into the client, Ruby Sumner. I talked briefly to her over the phone and so did Ava, and she sent me some contact information, but that's it."

Tahir cleared his throat. "The information I found is interesting, which only raises my suspicions."

"You're always suspicious," Hana interjected.

Alison silenced her with a stern look. "Go on, Tahir."

"The first thing I'll provide is what we can pretend is the good news. I can't find anything linking her to any underworld or terrorist group. If they're even aware of her, they've never stated so in either a positive or negative manner."

Mason frowned. "We can pretend that's the good news? That implies there's bad news which seriously undermines it."

"The bad news is that the woman barely exists."

"What do you mean?" Alison asked. "She sounded real enough when I talked to her."

"I mean she has a minimal electronic presence. A woman named Ruby Sumner does have an account at a local bank, but it was only established a week ago." He retrieved his phone and tapped it, and a holographic display of an attractive, dark-haired, pale-skinned woman in her twenties appeared above the table. "And she's conspicuously absent from a variety of government data-bases where one would expect a woman wealthy enough to hire Brownstone Security to at least appear. I've found other Ruby Sumners out there, but none of them are remotely near her age. There is no driver's license issued for anyone who looks like her in this country, Canada, or Mexico, and no ID card. The social security number asso-ciated with her newly opened bank account belongs to someone else entirely—a Cambodian-American woman who lives in Minnesota."

Hana rolled her eyes. "Sloppy."

"So she's a fraud." Mason frowned and drummed his fingers on the tabletop. "She's probably trying to use us to smuggle something for her and thinks that no one would dare mess with the Dark Princess. It's not a terrible plan, if overly obvious."

Tahir nodded. "That sounds right to me, but there's one small detail that makes me wonder."

Ava continued to take notes and barely glanced at the various employees of Brownstone Security.

"What is that?" Alison asked.

"Without a DNA sample for her, it'll be difficult to proceed deeper in terms of a background check, but I was curious and ran a basic image match to be thorough."

"An image match? Why?"

"Because you'd be surprised what you can find when you do that." He tapped his phone again and an additional image appeared beside the dark-haired woman. It was an identical, unsmiling woman in a black-and-white photograph, her hair up and in a high-necked, wide-skirted dress that looked like something from the nineteenth century—or something from Myna's closet.

"My algorithms indicate this image is a 99.5% match based on body type and face for the more modern image of the client," the infomancer explained. "The second photo was taken in 1884, and it's like she hasn't aged a day."

Hana gestured toward the older image. "I've seen this kind of thing before, though. Last week, I read this joke article where they tried to prove Jericho Cartwright was a wizard because they found pictures that looked like him from the 1800s and a painting that looked like him from the 1600s."

Tahir scoffed. "I doubt they used my algorithms."

"Stranger things have happened," Alison suggested. "There were many celebrities who came out as magicals once the gates opened and more than a few singers who were elves."

Mason shook his head. "But there's no reason for her to hide it. There are no rules against being a magical. Why would she hide it?"

"It's not impossible that she's a magical who wants to keep a low profile. Given everything we've all dealt with, we know that simply because it's not illegal or against some old rules to be a magical doesn't mean there aren't a huge number of problems." She glanced from one picture to the other. They did look like the same women, down to a mole on her cheek. "I don't know how I feel about this."

The life wizard frowned. "What's to feel? This woman is lying about who she is and refuses to tell you what she expects us to carry. It's too dangerous, and if the client won't trust us enough to tell the truth, that means there are other things she's probably kept from us."

Tahir nodded his agreement. Hana looked uncertain.

Alison scratched her cheek and tore her gaze away from the holographic doppelgangers. "I'm actually thinking about saying yes."

Everyone stared at her and waited in silence for an explanation.

"It's probably a trap," she explained finally.

"And?" Mason shrugged. "We should purposefully take a job that's a trap because we've gone a couple of weeks without anyone seriously attempting to kill us? Is this your way of trying to stay in shape?"

She shook her head. "What if it's a dark wizard plot? Because of Drysi's tip, things have picked up on our end and on Izzie's end too. We're breathing down their necks, and they might be worried that we're getting too close, so they're ready for a counteroffensive."

Tahir snorted. "Taking the job makes even less sense then. You're talking about walking into a trap set by an organization that has every reason to want you dead."

"If you know a trap is there, you can avoid it. And if it's supposed to be a secret, avoiding it might let you know who sprung it." She released a long sigh. "Maybe I'm wrong and it's nothing more than a smuggler, but my instincts tell me there's something more here—something we shouldn't overlook. I think we go in as a small team—only Hana, Mason, and myself with Tahir in remote support—and we see what we shake loose."

"What if it's nothing more than a bomb?" the info-mancer asked. "Sometimes, the most straight-forward plans can be the most successful."

"If they merely wanted to bomb me, they'd have more than enough opportunities. The wards and glyphs on the building and my condo might help to protect me, but I haven't warded all the streets to and from work, even if it were possible to do that. This seems a very elaborate way to kill me versus merely blowing up a city block when I happen to drive through it. It's not like they haven't proven that they don't care about innocent people dying."

"That still doesn't negate the possibility."

"You, Mason, and I can set up a containment spell," Alison suggested with a firm nod. "The client said it couldn't go through a portal, but she didn't say that no magic could be used near it. If we layer enough spells, it won't be a problem even if it does go off. Between the three of us, it'd be easy to set up decent containment spells on a small object in a contained area, even in a moving vehicle."

"You mean it *shouldn't* be a problem," Tahir smirked. "I'd only note that it's easy for me because I won't be physically present, but I'd prefer that Hana not be blown up."

The fox laughed. "That'd be nice. I still have to name my new dog."

His smirk vanished, and he shook his head and avoided her challenging look. "It's still a risk."

The half-Drow sighed. "I know it is, and that's why I'm involved, too. But I don't want to walk away if it's a chance to turn the tables on someone who is messing with us. I won't force anyone to do it, though."

Mason shrugged. "If you're in, I'm in."

Hana nodded. "I'm in too."

"It's easy for me to agree," Tahir replied. "I won't even be there."

Alison smiled. "Then it's time for the Brownstone Security to try their hand at being an armed courier service."

CHAPTER SIX

The Brownstone security team stepped out of the armored SUV at the corner of a shopping center parking lot. A pale man in a dark suit with slick hair stood in the center of an empty parking space. He gave off an undertaker vibe, and the look on his face suggested that smiling was a foreign idea.

Yeah, this isn't suspicious at all.

Alison walked over to the man, alert for obvious trouble, but her quick scrutiny of the area revealed no other cars nearby, including any obvious transportation for him. "Mr. Dennison. You look exactly like your pictures."

He nodded. "As it should be, and I also hope that my reputation precedes me, Miss Brownstone. I would hate to have to waste time explaining my role here, but from your reputation, I imagine I don't need to."

"Yeah. I know who you are."

She had heard of him before, and his presence made the entire situation even more suspicious. Dennison didn't work for anyone directly. He was a professional middle-man for people who needed high-value objects handled in all manner of exchanges, both legal and illegal. Everyone from the Mafia to the PDA occasionally made use of his services.

While she hadn't used Dennison before, a few of her clients had hired similar men. Although she had a strict policy against working for anonymous people, she had no issue with those who didn't want to physically meet her. Everyone had their reasons.

This particular client had been more than willing to talk to Alison and Ava directly, but given what Tahir had found, it was entirely possible that the woman on the phone wasn't what she appeared.

Is that why she doesn't want to meet me directly? Because she's worried I'll discover what she really is? And why does this guy have to look so gaunt and pale? He's like a well-dressed corpse. Seriously, he looks less like an undertaker than like the undertaker's client.

Dennison gestured a little impatiently. "For your information, I've already handled the object to verify its general touch safety, and I am prepared to bring it to you contingent upon your agreement to take the job. I also saw the client and her people handle it by direct touch, and she's assured me the only restriction is that it can't go through a portal. She was very, very clear on that point."

"What happens if goes through a portal?" Hana asked. "Does it explode?"

"Oh no, my dear." He shook his head. "Nothing so unfortunate, and the client also promised me that's not the case. The issue is one of damage to her property, not the surrounding area. The object inside will be ruined if transported via portal magic. In addition, exposure to light can also damage it, so she has sealed it with a number of spells to ensure that it won't be opened easily without knowing the appropriate spells or a tremendous amount of magical effort. She has also noted that the magic will ensure that she'll know if it has been tampered with. You are strictly forbidden to open it, and it's my understanding that she already explained that."

Alison nodded. "She mentioned something like that, yeah."

I wonder how many couriers deal with this kind of thing long-term. I'm not used to flying so blind on a job. It'd be annoying to never know if I carried a rare collectible coin or an ancient Oriceran WMD.

The thought of that made her grimace. She could see herself going back to bounty hunting but never being a full-time courier.

"Please note," Dennison added, and boredom underlaid his tone and infected his expression, "that any issues with the condition of the delivery must be taken up with the client. I simply deliver the information and goods provided to me. It's also my understanding that she has provided you with an address in Portland. If you have not received that information, I need to know right away to pass it along to her. You are, of course, free to deal with her directly as per her instructions, but I would prefer to make sure there are fewer issues with the delivery on either end. It saves trouble later if blame must be assigned."

"That's a cheery thought," she replied a little caustically.

The man shrugged, his movement infused with weary annoyance. "It's a product of years of experience, Miss

Brownstone. Please don't take offense or perceive it as a particular reflection of my belief in your personal skills."

She gestured dismissively. "Honestly, I don't really care. And, yeah, the client already gave me the details. I assume, based on the address, that the box isn't super-heavy, right? Because she wants us to take it into the kemana, and it's not exactly possible to drive a car into one."

He shook his head. "The box is as light as a pixie. I'm to formally specify that there are dangerous elements who are interested in the contents of this box. The client has no specific intelligence on threats that might attack you, but she did make it clear to me that it was a distinct possibility. These aforementioned dangerous elements are more than likely to consist of magicals with combat training."

Alison chuckled. "She was a little less clear on that part, but I suppose it makes sense why she needs us, rather than a more conventional high-value courier. It's not a big deal. We're a security company. We protect people and things all the time."

Dennison's nod was almost imperceptible. "The client, of course, will demand a refund if the package is destroyed along the way, either through breakage and exposure to light or through conventional damage."

Hana snorted. "Who do you think you're dealing with? We're not a bunch of amateurs she hired off the Internet."

He waggled a finger in protest. "I'm simply passing along what I was told, Miss Sugimoto. I have no strong feelings on it either way. Let me be clear about that once again." He withdrew his phone. "If you wish to refuse the job at this time, you may do so. I'm personally unaware of the contents of the package, but it has been emphasized to me that it is better off not in the hands of objectionable elements. Use that information as you will. If you have any additional questions, feel free to ask them of me at this time or contact the client, but be aware that I'll be the one to pass the package to you in Seattle."

Alison looked at Hana and Mason. They both nodded. There wasn't anything else she could think of that would be of importance.

"We'll take the job," she confirmed.

"Excellent." Dennison rubbed his hands together. "I'll contact you with the pick-up address tomorrow morning one hour before our meeting time. Please don't be late. If you are, I will depart and inform the client."

"Don't worry. We'll be there."

Mason drummed his fingers on the SUV steering wheel as they pulled out of the parking lot. "If I wasn't convinced this was a trap before, I'm definitely convinced now. I don't know if it could scream trap louder without a mic connected to speakers turned up to the maximum and enhanced with an amplification spell. Are you sure about this, A?"

Alison laughed from the front passenger seat. "Definitely. The only thing is that the more details we get, the less I'm convinced it's the Seventh Order. This isn't their style at all. It's almost...too subtle and using men like Dennison provides a trail that can be followed. He might be a middle-man, but he takes precautions to make sure people don't screw other people over and blame him."

"Who then?" He narrowed his eyes, the suspicion on his face almost infectious.

"I don't know. It's a big list. I'd say definitely not New Veil or HDL. They wouldn't be able to keep it together long enough to play with someone like Dennison. Whoever it is has to be a magical or have access to magicals because they must know we'll check the box immediately to determine if it's magic."

Hana folded her arms in the back seat. "My money's on Scott. I'm sure he has enough money squirreled away in accounts here and there that he can set something up. It's not that hard to find a few wizard mercenaries to enchant a box."

"From the inside of an ultramax where he's being heavily monitored?" Alison shook her head. "He's impressive, but I doubt he can pull that stunt off, and it's also not his style. If he wanted revenge, he had plenty of time to set it up. He said his piece to the world and did his little experiment. Chesterton, maybe, but the same applies, and he wasn't as subtle as Scott, to begin with."

She snorted. "The truth is we've made a lot of noise in our time in Seattle, not to mention in places like Japan or Nereid Island. There could be a number of different groups trying to set it up. The one thing I will say, though, is that the fact they have a middle-man like Dennison involved means they're trying to maintain a distance between them and us. Still, it probably won't be something as crude as a bomb. Involving another person merely means someone who might point my dad, for example, at them if something nasty happens and I end up dead."

"So it's a trap, but they don't want us dead?"

"Not necessarily. I'm only saying they need a situation that isn't we pick the package up and it goes boom. It's too obvious. It'll probably be an attack along the way."

Mason changed lanes and his gaze lingered on the rearview mirror for a few almost paranoid seconds. "Maybe we should have both Tahir and Sonya provide support on this one. It wouldn't hurt to have maximum eyes watching our backs."

"No. Sonya's getting good practice supporting Jerry's team, and I don't want to pull her off since we don't really have anyone else to support them. After that job last week, I've become convinced she's a big asset for Jerry and his men. Plus, it helps her to build up some pride without Tahir always looking over her shoulder." Alison pulled her phone out and entered the destination address and pick-up address. "At decent, law-abiding speeds, it'll take us about three and a half hours to reach the destination. Add a little time to take the box inside and drop it off but even then, it's not a lengthy job. We can be back Seattle in time for victory sushi if it isn't a trap."

"If we take the chopper, we can do it in an hour," the life wizard suggested. "A faster time means less time for the bad guys to get the drop on us, and they might not even have aircraft. It also leaves more time for sushi."

Alison grinned at him. "You're bound and determined to crash my helicopter, aren't you? You don't have to do that to impress me."

"Come on, A. You know what I mean. You can't fly as fast or as far as the helicopter, and we can't speed in one of the SUVs without the cops stopping us. It's an option."

"If I am shot down when I fly, the only thing that will

hit the ground is one body." She frowned. "A helicopter means more of a mess. You're a great pilot, but you're also a great driver, and I think you'll have an easier time controlling a crashing car than a crashing helicopter. Nope." She nodded curtly. "We stick to the original plan. We'll take an SUV for pick-up and delivery. We'll maintain and recharge our shields throughout the drive, despite the strain, and we'll reinforce the package as well in case it does turn out to be a bomb."

Hana licked her lips nervously. "And if we're ambushed on the road?"

"I doubt they'll make a big show of doing it on the I-5 with so many other cars around." She looked over her shoulder at her friend. "The more of a commotion they make, the more likely it is that the authorities will show up." She frowned at her phone and brought up a map of their journey. "Hmm. I doubt there are any AET teams in the cities between us and Portland, so we have a couple of hours in which we're vulnerable. Otherwise, this should be a straight-forward job."

"Except for the very real chance that someone will attack us," Mason pointed out wryly.

She grinned. "Why do you think we'll do this in one of the company SUVs rather than my Fiat?"

CHAPTER SEVEN

The next morning, Mason hauled a black glyph-covered box to the back of the SUV. Dennison had summoned them to an empty pier. The only other signs of life nearby were a few elves on a small raft that skimmed across the water, propelled by a spell.

I hope this package isn't a bomb, Alison thought.

The box didn't suggest that, but then again, most magical bombs didn't. It wasn't like she could expect obvious electronics or explosives. Magic made the impossible possible, and that included the most innocuous objects becoming deadly.

The more I think about it, a strange glyph-covered box is probably what the average magical bomb looks like, actually.

She layered another shield over herself. Hana's skin glowed light-red from her crystal ring, and Mason had increased his own protection before picking the box up.

They'd already activated their barriers as a precaution. Dennison lingered near their SUV, so at least if they were blown up, he'd go with them. For some reason, that comforted her. Perhaps because there was something almost arrogant in his nonchalance.

The wizard set the box gently in the back of the SUV before he secured it with straps. "It's not heavy at all, and nothing rolled or shifted as I walked."

Alison stepped closer to inspect the mysterious package. The solid black looked metallic and was cool to the touch. The entire thing was marginally bigger than a shoebox, with similar dimensions. She narrowed her eyes as she traced the glyphs that lined the sides and top with her gaze.

No. Wait. Do I really see what I think I see?

"That's interesting," she muttered. "Very interesting, and it might explain a few things."

Mason secured the last strap. "What is it, A? What do you see?"

Hana tilted her head and sniffed at the air. "Definitely magic."

The half-Drow pointed at one of the glyphs. "Do you recognize this?"

He peered at it and shook his head. "Huh. Actually, I don't. It looks like a glyph for a containment ward, but I can't say I've ever seen one like this before. There are differences in the design that should mess it up. At least, if I tried to cast a ward using this glyph, it wouldn't work. They aren't my specialty, though."

She regretted not bringing Tahir along to help secure the package now that it was in front of her. The more magicals the better would have been the safer course of action. "I have. I recognize it. In fact, I recognize all of them."

He frowned. "You do?"

Hana wandered over, her hand on the hilt of her *tachi* in its sheath. "Is there a problem?"

Alison pointed to the glyph and then a few others. "What about these, Mason? Any ideas?"

He took a little more time to examine them closely. "Same thing. I can vaguely tell what I think they're supposed to be, but they're very different than what I'm used to. A couple of them, I don't recognize at all. That's rare. I usually have at least some clue. The general principles of glyphs should apply, right?"

"Not necessarily. After all, it varies depending on the type of magic used to fuel them." She took a few deep breaths and her heart rate lurched into a gallop. "And you don't recognize them because they're Drow glyphs."

Mason jerked back from the box. "What?"

Hana's eyes widened. "Are you sure?" She looked around as if a horde of Dark Elves might appear and lay waste to Seattle.

I don't know if I should be offended or not. Maybe they think one Dark Princess is enough for the city, and I can't say I disagree.

"Oh, I'm sure these are Drow. One hundred percent sure." Alison shook her head. "Trust me. I spent years at the School of Necessary Magic learning standard ward and glyph techniques, and Myna has spent hours showing me how to refine them to work better with my Drow shadow magic. Not every glyph on this box is Drow, but a lot of them are." She spun and marched over to the eerily calm Dennison. "If this is stolen Drow property, I won't transport it. The client didn't say anything about the Drow to me. Neither did you."

He released a long, weary sigh. "I can't verify that it's not stolen or if the box belongs to the Drow in some cosmic legal sense."

"That's some fine parsing." Her nostrils flared. "But there's something you can verify, then?"

The intermediary gave another tiny nod. "Yes. I was told this box and the property inside belonged to the client. I verified that with a truth spell. I'm willing to submit to a truth spell so you can, in turn, verify what I know. The client wasn't a Drow—or, at least, she didn't identify herself as such or resemble one."

Alison took a few deep breaths. She needed more information before she could determine how to react. "The box belongs to the client? A box covered with Drow glyphs?"

Dennison nodded. "Indeed. That's all I can verify. If you intend to refuse delivery, I would prefer you to do it now."

"It's fine," she spat. "We'll spend time casting containment spells. There's no reason for you to stick around. Consider it officially on delivery."

The next half-hour passed in a blur as Mason and Alison worked together to layer containment spells over the box. It might have been overkill and a waste of magical energy, but it was better than blowing up halfway through the trip to Portland or accidentally opening a hole to the World in Between.

Hana sat in the back, the long *tachi* at her feet. Mason drove and Alison stared out the window as she struggled to untangle the meaning of the glyphs.

Drow glyphs. Of course they are Drow glyphs.

He glanced quickly at her. "It was bound to happen, A. I wouldn't get too worried about it."

Alison looked over at him. "What?"

"It was inevitable that a Drow would hire you at some point. This explains why they used the middle-man. They must have known you'd see it immediately if they showed up face to face." He shrugged before he changed lanes.

"Drow shadow magic does have a certain flavor," she replied. "But why hide it? If it's not stolen, why would they play this game with Dennison and conceal their identity?"

"It's a test," Hana suggested. She nodded her head definitively after a moment. "Definitely a test."

"What do you mean?"

"Not every Drow's like Myna, right?"

Alison frowned. "Considering how old she is, no. I still don't understand what you mean, though."

The other woman gestured widely with her hands. "I only meant that she hasn't been to Earth in hundreds of years, but other Drow have visited. You wouldn't be here if they hadn't. They have every reason to establish connections and a power base here. Just because King Oriceran runs the planet doesn't mean they want to support everything the Light Elves do."

The fox was right. Alison had underestimated the Drow. She was so used to Myna being clueless about modern society that she'd let herself forget that not every Drow had avoided Earth for centuries. The assassins who had targeted her father had no trouble adjusting to or operating in LA, after all.

Mason's right. This was inevitable.

She snickered. "True enough, but my mom was a special case. I see what you mean, though. That also explains Ruby Sumner. I don't have natural Drow shapeshifting, but all full-blooded Drow do. So, what you're saying is that the Drow are moving some sort of item, but they've run afoul of someone and decided to let the half-breed princess take the heat for them?"

"It sounds reasonable," Tahir replied, his voice clear through her ear receiver.

The response startled her. The infomancer had been so quiet during the last half-hour that she'd forgotten he was there.

"Reasonable?" she asked. "How does that work, exactly?"

"Yes," Tahir confirmed. "Everything you've told us about the Drow and Myna suggests an obsession with martial strength. It's as you noted. Your reputation is growing, and if the Drow have a reason to otherwise keep a low profile, it wouldn't hurt to have a fellow Drow aid them while simultaneously verifying your prowess in battle against Earth magical groups. I wouldn't be surprised if they have purposefully picked a fight with some local magicals or Oriceran immigrants as a baseline test of a powerful Drow versus possible enemies."

"But that doesn't tell us who might want to steal the box. I doubt it's a group of Light Elves or gnomes. Of course, that's not impossible. There are some fucked-up Light Elves and gnomes out there too."

That was the problem with Oriceran. It was a world of wonder and magic, but it was also a world of terror and danger with countless intelligent races who all had their own agendas. The Great Treaty might have kept world-shattering war from sweeping across the planet, but it didn't ensure that no race ever interfered with another.

Alison glanced into the back. The straps and the spells kept the box secure. "If the Drow are behind this, it means it probably isn't a bomb. No Drow will rely on something as indirect as a bomb to eliminate me, so the idea that they're using me to screw with someone else makes more sense. My question is who did they piss off, or who are they *trying* to piss off? Myna's not a good source of intelligence for something like this. When I visited them last, I didn't hear that they had any particular trouble with anyone on Earth—not that they were all that interested in giving me much inside information on their plans."

Hana shrugged. "Does it really matter? A job's a job, right? Whether the guys fighting us are terrorists, oni, or mercenaries with power armor is irrelevant."

"True enough." The half-Drow sighed. "Tahir, make sure no one ambushes us. I'd hate for the Drow to go back to Oriceran to snicker about the Princess of the Shadow Forged defeated like an idiot." Dark clouds loomed on the horizon and rain was sure to follow. It was hardly unexpected in western Washington in October but definitely inconvenient.

Tahir chuckled quietly. "I'll strive to ensure your reputation remains intact—or at least provide you the opportunity to achieve that yourself."

Alison leaned back in her seat. It wasn't like she ever forgot that she was a Drow. Her nickname, Dark Princess, was a constant reminder of her heritage, along with her white hair, even if her skin hadn't darkened. Her powers and her Drow mentor also only reinforced that.

Despite all that, she hadn't had direct dealings with the rest of the Dark Elves since her visit to Oriceran, and she didn't want to. The more she dealt with them, the more she risked being drawn into their complicated politics and a world she had no interest in.

I hope this doesn't turn into a big mess, but every time I hope for something like that, I never get my wish.

Shit. What will I do if a bunch of royal guard Light Elves show up?

"Have you had any luck on solving the mystery of your dog?" she asked, desperate to force her mind off an uncontrollable worry. She wouldn't be able to make a decision until she ran into an enemy, so there really was no point in worrying about it.

"No one has answered any of my inquiries, and I've not found any missing animals report matching the creature," Tahir stated gloomily.

Hana laughed. "He loves the dog but doesn't want to admit it. Today's the big test, though. I bought a little temporary pen for him the other night, and I'm curious to see how he reacts. I have paper laid out for him since there is no way he can hold it all day."

"Maybe you should ask around more in the magical community," Alison suggested. "If the dog is some kind of Oriceran animal, they might know."

The fox shrugged and looked unimpressed with the idea. "I'll think about it. How is house hunting going? I haven't heard you mention it in a few days."

Mason snorted from the driver's seat. "Slowly."

The half-Drow laughed. "It's not that bad. We're having trouble finding the best place for all our needs."

"Make sure it's magic dog-friendly," Hana insisted. "You never know when we might want to visit."

"I'll keep that in mind. Let's get through today and then we can both go back to worrying about our search for dog owners and new homes."

CHAPTER EIGHT

The SUV's wipers worked furiously to sweep the water away from the windshield. Heavy raindrops pounded the glass, and the wind combined with the speed of the vehicle to spread the deluge in what amounted to a water shotgun blast.

Some days, in this state, I regret not starting my business in Death Valley, Alison thought.

Powerful gusts threatened to shove the SUV off the road, but Mason managed solid control of the vehicle. They maintained their lane position even though there was no one else around, but for all they knew, someone could rocket past at any second. It had happened more than once already.

The dark clouds turned day almost into night, the sun now obscured and little more than a distant memory. He stuck to the speed limit rather than test what might happen when an armored SUV with three magicals aboard ended up in a massive highway accident.

They had already passed one empty car that had

crashed into a guard rail. The driver was long gone, though, so thankfully, no one had needed assistance.

Alison frowned. At least they had an advantage in that there seemed to be far more cars heading north than south on the highway that morning. The traffic density difference lowered the chance of both an accident and of innocent people caught up in any possible incident.

Now that she knew the Drow were involved as clients, she doubted that they would be able to make it all the way to Portland without some trouble. Still, the awful weather should prevent any surprises in the form of dropships or helicopters. That offered a little comfort in the general unease that came with knowing nothing about what lay ahead.

As if reading his girlfriend's thoughts, Mason snorted. "And I wanted to go up in this."

"You would have checked the weather." She shrugged. "It's no big deal."

"This is a nasty storm. Far nastier than they predicted."

There really was no point in even trying to answer that. The initial re-opening of the gates, besides allowing magic to begin to leak back into Earth, had also led to strange and transient effects on the weather. Although most major weather patterns weren't wildly different than decades before, a bizarre storm might occasionally arise with little explanation. When magic was active, it was far harder for science to firmly forecast everything that might occur. Whether it was mere chance or the pernicious effects of magic, anyone who lived in western Washington was prepared to deal with a nasty wind storm.

"There's a minor issue, Alison," Tahir reported, a faint hint of tension in his voice.

"What's wrong? And does it involve anything exploding?" She straightened immediately, her shoulder stiff. She glanced into the rear and side mirrors for any suspicious vehicles. Distant headlights cut through the torrents of rain, but the vehicle responsible didn't appear to move closer.

Are they keeping their distance, or is it no one special at all? I would attack in the middle of a storm, but I doubt they planned it so well.

"I anticipated the issue with the rain and put some additional spells on my drone, but if this weather keeps up, I'll lose it despite feeding more magic into it," he explained. "The drone might survive, but there is lightning further north in the storm system. The gusts and lightning activity will be heavy and, from what I can tell, will persist all the way down to Cowlitz County. I can't shield a drone well enough to take a direct lightning strike."

Alison frowned. All the way down to Cowlitz County? That meant they might have to endure bad weather all the way to the Oregon border, which was not optimal when they tried to maintain backup reconnaissance and avoid ambushes from the shadows.

"Damn it." She sucked in a breath and thought the implications over. "But if you can't keep a drone up, that means the enemy probably can't either. If they are non-infomancers, they might not bother, but we have a few anti-tracking wards up at the moment to handle that. Do your best and keep your drone up there as long as you can."

New rule, I guess. No jobs when there might be heavy rain. Wait. That means we wouldn't work for half the year.

She smirked a little at the thought.

They had been driving for a while now and cruised past another exit. All the upcoming exits would take them into Centralia, hardly a bustling metropolis. The small number of police that patrolled the small town would have no chance against a serious magical.

Alison considered that. Many magicals had come from Oriceran or become more active with the start of the return of magic. While everyone focused on the flashy elves, gnomes, and other races that poured into human cities, many creatures preferred the wilderness. A powerful magical might be able to wreak havoc in a small city, but to what end?

I'd better not bring trouble to any place along the way, no matter what happens, but I also can't have a major battle on the highway. It's too damned risky.

She drew a deep, calming breath. Their journey was far from over. The box in the back remained closed and quiet, and no enemies had appeared to launch attacks. They might be lucky and pass the next few hours with nothing more than tense but otherwise unremarkable driving.

Lightning flashed in the distance from multiple directions and the overlapping rumbles vibrated through the car. Another bolt struck far ahead. It was like the work of an angry, ancient god who laid waste to the false temples of the mortals below. If it hadn't already rained on and off for the last few weeks, she would have worried about forest fires.

"This is great kite flying weather," Hana declared with a laugh. "I wish I had brought one."

Alison grinned and a little of her tension dissipated at her friend's joke. "It is at that. There was this one time in college when I participated in a magic kite flying demonstration. It wasn't flashy. Mostly, I generated wind to do weird stunts. It was a weird period all round, actually. I spent most of college still obsessed with dark wizards and bounty hunting, but every once in a while, I did let myself remember that fun was a thing."

"Really? You could have become Alison Brownstone, Empress of All Kites rather than Dark Princess of Ass-Kicking."

She laughed at the thought. "I don't think I could have ended up doing something like that. Between my parents and what happened at the School of Necessary Magic, I was unfortunately destined to do something a little more…tough."

"Who knows?" Hana's smile was coy. "I thought I'd be nothing but a cheap con artist my entire life, and here I am, a security contractor traveling the world." She gestured to the sword at her feet. "And I run around with a magic super-sword from the world's most dangerous former tomb raider turned college professor."

"Good point." Alison released a wistful sigh. "I can't say I'm unhappy with where I've ended up, but it's hard not to think how different things might have been. Maybe I think more about this lately because Mom's pregnant. I wonder if my little brother or sister will end up another tough Brownstone, or—I don't know, a flighty artist or something."

"I would hate to be the art critic who dared criticize a Brownstone's painting." Her friend winked and both women laughed.

Mason kept his hands firmly on the wheel, his mouth rigid, and the mirth had no effect on him at all. Tension lined his forehead. "This wind is crazy, and the storm is battering us hard." His gaze flicked between the rearview mirror and the rear camera. "At this rate, anyone following us will have to survive the storm before they have a hope of taking a shot at us." His expression softened. "I don't know if that's a good thing or a bad thing."

Hana yawned and stretched her arms to her sides. "We're all shielded, one way or another. We'll survive a wreck. Not that I want to sit outside in the middle of a major storm waiting for a tow truck and a rideshare."

"There's trouble," Tahir declared and sounded a mixture of annoyed and angry. "The drone's down. It's been destroyed."

"Lightning?" Alison asked and incredulity crept into her voice.

Well, at least I had a little relaxation before work came calling.

"Unfortunately, I don't think it's the weather. I was doing a good job of keeping it stable with additional magic. Something struck it from below. It was very quick and although I've isolated the frame with the attack, I can't really distinguish what struck it. It's a very dark shape and could be one of a number of different projectiles or attack types."

She cracked her knuckles. "That answers that. Someone noticed and bothered to take out your drone. It's either the world's angriest anti-drone fanatic thinking the storm will cover him, or someone who wants to cause trouble without anyone recording it. It could even be someone who followed us in the distance from before the storm started. That would explain how they knew to take out the drone."

"All valid possibilities," the infomancer replied. "Next time, I'll send a whole fleet of mechanicals."

"It's okay. It's not like we didn't expect this. If anything, they screwed up. Now we know they're coming." She scoffed at the apparent stupidity of the enemy. "Which means they're careful enough to take out potential witnesses but too arrogant to care about warning us."

"They might not have realized that the drone was associated with you," he pointed out.

"Huh. That's true, too. I guess I'm merely spoiling for a fight."

Mason's nostrils flared. "How do you want to play this, A?"

"Tahir, about how far back was your drone?" she asked and her gaze flicked to the side as distant high beams cut through the heavy rain.

"About two hundred feet back and as high up," he replied. "It didn't tumble. By that I mean it was destroyed instantly by whatever struck it."

"Damn. That means whoever did it is probably a lot closer than I would like."

"A good assumption."

Alison frowned as she considered the tactical possibilities. At least the roads were all but empty. She assumed the high beams were from whoever had annihilated the drone.

"Our first move should be to get off the highway." She pointed at the GPS display on the console. "Without the drone coverage and the storm, if it is some angry anti-Drow magicals, they might not hesitate to blow up anyone near them to make their point." She tapped the map.

Mason's gaze darted there before it returned to the rain-drenched road in front. "What about it?"

"We can get off the highway at the next exit and follow the side road to the right. It should take us to some trees beside the river. Go ahead and floor it, Mason."

"Huh? We'll try to outrun them? I don't get it. They'll be able to find us in the trees."

"That's as good as place as any to make a stand." She shook her head. "And I need five or ten seconds for my plan. I'll try to surprise them while they think about surprising us."

The wizard pressed the accelerator. The SUV increased speed…eighty…eighty-five…ninety… Ninety-five…at this speed, if there had been any other cars on the slick road, a collision would have been unavoidable. The exit delivered them smoothly down a side road.

Mason jerked the wheel, the tires squealed, and they hydroplaned for several yards. He completed his final turn toward the dark trees that loomed in the distance. The vehicle shuddered when it left the road and mud splattered the side windows.

He pressed lightly on the brakes. Impact with the trees wasn't in the plan, and the muddy road didn't slow their momentum rapidly enough. Behind them, the high beams from before turned in their direction. They were definitely being followed.

The SUV passed a few of the outer trees and slowed before it finally ground to a halt near multiple trunks that grew close together. The swollen river raged not all that far away.

"Okay, A," he declared. "Now what?"

"Time for a little aerial surprise," Alison replied. "You guys hold their attention." She threw the door open and exited the vehicle with a grimace as her boots sank into the mud. Shadow wings burst from her back, and she soared high. The heavy wind buffeted her, and she gritted her teeth with the effort to maintain her position.

The high beams from three cars converged on the parked SUV. Dark sedans pulled off the road onto the muddy track and continued toward the trees as Mason and Hana stepped out of the vehicle.

Glowing tails and red skin highlighted the fox in the rain as she raised her dangerous blade. Headlights glinted off the weapon and lent an eerie cast to her rosy aura. Alison struggled against the storm but managed to hover about fifty feet above the vehicles. The sedans slowed to a stop.

Don't notice me, assholes.

Her teammates advanced slowly toward the three cars.

The doors opened, and a total of eight men and women piled out of each. They neither drew nor wielded any weapons, and there was nothing informative or even uniform about their clothing from a distance. Some wore jeans and T-shirts, while others wore suits. One woman was dressed incongruously in a rather unseasonable floral sundress and heels.

Yeah, that's not suspicious at all.

There also wasn't a single wand in sight. That narrowed the possibilities down.

Alison floated lower. If anyone sensed the magic above them, they gave no indication of it. The new arrivals all focused on Mason and Hana. It was great when a plan actually worked.

Okay, not witches or wizards, but they could be almost anyone or anything using disguise magic. For all I know, it's a swarm of dragons.

Their forms blurred for a moment. She frowned and squinted intently at the group. Her first thought was that the storm-driven rain had disrupted her vision, but her stomach tightened when she realized this wasn't the case at all.

The new arrivals had transformed. Their jet-black skin blended with the shadows, but their stark white hair provided an easy target on which to focus.

Drow. The realization was confirmed when shadow blades extended from their arms. A dark nimbus surrounded them.

Shit. That explains it. There is no hidden enemy. No royal guard. We ended up in the middle of Drow versus Drow crap. Fucking wonderful.

CHAPTER NINE

Mason raised his fists and Hana her sword, both grim-faced and ready to fight.

Shit, shit, shit, she thought.

Despite all the trouble with Laena years before, Alison had left the Drow on good terms after training with them. The last thing she needed was to start another round of the Oricerans Screw with Brownstone game.

Her dad had once had to basically nuke three of them to stop them from flooding an area with dangerous monsters because the damned Drow refused to lose with any sense of grace. While she doubted the eight new arrivals were as powerful as Laena's personal elite squad, they were probably equally poor losers.

Her time on Oriceran had taught her that. Drow pride was an impressive power in and of itself.

She flew toward Hana and Mason and dropped directly in front of them but kept her wings extended. Her boots sank into the muddy ground. It wasn't her preferred battlefield, but her foes would have the same disadvantage.

"Stop right there," she bellowed. The howling wind demanded it. "I don't think the Guardians would appreciate you wandering around on Earth picking random fights."

One of the men scowled at her. "Alison Brownstone, the Princess of the Shadow Forged."

"That's me." She extended a shadow blade. "But like I said, what about the Guardians?"

"Fools who cling to power they don't deserve," the Drow scoffed. "And this isn't a random fight. This is a Drow matter."

"What are you? A pack of royalists?"

"It's not your concern." He raised his chin, the disdain in his eyes obvious. "You chose Earth, not Oriceran. You chose humans, not your people. You're not Drow. You're merely a human with some Drow powers."

Alison's face twitched. The words had cut deeper than she expected. "I don't really give a crap what you think of me, but you have a few questions to answer since you've followed me and now, a whole squad of you is here, threatening me and my friends."

Lightning flashed in the distance and highlighted the vehicles in vivid relief. Someone remained inside—a dark-haired woman, her features obscured by the rain and distance.

"We don't have to answer any questions," the Drow sneered. "Especially from a princess who runs from her duty. The opinions of the Guardians are irrelevant. They are on Oriceran, and we're here with you. The only Drow you should care about are those right in front of you."

So much for the royalty card and the politics card. I'm too used to Myna's respect. Fine. We'll deal with this using the only other language the Drow understand.

She snorted her derision. "This isn't about me being a Drow princess. This is about me being Alison Brownstone, President and CEO of Brownstone Security—and the woman who sealed a Mountain Strider, among other things. I have a long list of victories I could brag about, but the question you really need to ask yourself is whether you think you could all win against me if I was on my own, let alone with help. Because I have to say, I sincerely doubt it."

He pointed his shadow blade at her. "You will turn the box over. Spare us your cheap threats."

Alison shook her head. "The box isn't stolen. The owner of that box has paid me to ensure it's delivered, and so I don't see a reason to hand it over to some random rude Drow."

"Are you so sure it's not stolen?" he sneered.

Shit. I don't think Dennison was lying, but if someone got their hands on a truthbender, they might have purposefully set him up to screw with me. I thought I could avoid the worst of the trap by walking directly into it, but maybe I screwed up and made it worse. Not that I'll let these assholes know that.

Nothing has forced them into a confrontation. If this really is some Drow pre-civil war crap, I have to be careful. But I also have to let them know right here and now that they can't fuck with me. Otherwise, it'll never be over.

Mason and Hana remained ready to strike, their knees slightly bent and their gazes never wavering from the line of adversaries, regardless of the lightning flashing in the background.

"You know what?" Alison responded, squared her

shoulders, and injected confidence into her voice. "Let me put it another way. I'm sure enough that it's not stolen to kick your asses all the way back to Oriceran if you try to take it. I don't care whether you recognize my authority as Princess of the Shadow Forged or not, but you will recognize my authority as a powerful magical who is willing to fight to defend my client's property. You'll also recognize the power and authority of my two top people."

Mason tilted his chin, a slight smirk on his face. Hana's grin was so vicious, it was very likely that she'd spent hours practicing it in the mirror.

A small amount of the Drow's arrogance drained from his face. "We don't want to hurt you, Princess, or your friends, but we have our orders, and we need that box. You might be a powerful warrior, but there are eight of us and only three of you. You must realize that whatever power you think you have, it doesn't mean you can defeat a large number of powerful foes."

Mason scoffed. "If you have any intelligence agents or spies, fire them right away. They are not doing a good job."

Hana laughed, a crazed gleam in her eye. "The way I see it, eight of you and three of us means that effectively, we outnumber you two to one. Maybe even four to one." She switched to a bad English accent. "Hardly sporting, old chaps!"

The Drow's brow furrowed in irritation. "You seem to be confused about the power of our warriors. We're not common human scum like you're accustomed to dealing with."

The fox snickered and her tails swished behind her, the glow refracted in the rain. "I work for a Drow princess. I think I understand the power of a Drow. Except, here's the thing—she's the one backing me, and unless you have a Drow princess in your little group there, you don't stand a chance."

Mason nodded, pride on his face. "She has a point."

Alison pointed her shadow blade at the challenger. "You said you don't want to hurt me. The same thing applies for me to you. I don't know you, and I have no desire to hurt you, but I was paid to deliver this object. I'm not a courier, so you need to convince me to give it up if you don't want to fight me. If it's something dangerous, maybe we can discuss it, but you'll have to submit to a truth spell and prove you don't have a truthbender on you."

He shook his head. "You don't need to know what is in the box. That's Drow business. You merely need to give it to me. This is your last chance."

Hana snapped the fingers of her free hand. "Did you hear that? He's using *your* line. Oh, it's so on. You're in for some pain now, Mr. Drow."

All eight elves took a step back as Alison layered a few more shields over herself. A few cast nervous looks at her.

So you do understand what I can do, huh?

"If you're unwilling to give me more information," she explained coldly, "that limits your options. Option one, you get back in your cars and drive the hell away. With that one, there's the added bonus that no one dies. Option two, we fight and some of you might die. I don't want to kill any of you, but I won't risk my people's lives to protect yours if you attack us. You're Drow. You should know better than to go up against a Drow princess and expect to emerge unscathed."

The leader glared at her. "You have such confidence. Don't think because you spent a small amount of time training on Oriceran you're ready to defeat us."

"It has nothing to do with that and everything to do with the fact that I grow more powerful all the time. I'm not the same scared little girl Laena tried to abduct." She released her wings and funneled shadow magic to her legs. "And right now, I don't see you as Drow. I see you as petty thieves trying to steal the rightful property of my client. This is your last chance, asshole."

"Thieves?" He gritted his teeth. "How dare you! You're nothing but a half-human who shouldn't have any claim to the title of Princess of the Shadow Forged. You've forfeited your right to your heritage."

"I'll show you why I have that title, asshole," Alison replied with a mocking grin. "Mason, Hana, don't go for their heads. We don't need to kill them. We merely need to teach them a lesson. The more who survive, the more who can go back to Oriceran and explain why screwing with me is a terrible idea."

"You'll pay for that, Brownstone." Her adversary rushed toward her and raised his shadow blade.

She released the energy in her legs and launched herself toward the center of the Drow formation. Hana and Mason charged on opposite sides and their rapid footsteps churned low arcs of mud behind them.

The half-Drow sliced with her blade. The strike knocked her opponent back but didn't penetrate his protection, although his eyes widened and his shield dimmed.

The momentum of the blow spun her away. She

extended a shadow tentacle into the muddy ground to anchor herself and swing her toward a nearby woman for a follow-up attack.

Hana's movement was almost a blur as she pounded into the flank of the Drow line. Her quick strikes forced a warrior back and the *tachi* weakened his shield with each blow. Mason closed on the enemy from the other side and his lightning-fast charged punches drove his target back with relentless force.

The Drow leader tried to stab Alison as she hacked at her current victim, but she forced more power into her blade and ducked to easily avoid his attack. Her next slice penetrated his shield and cut deep into his abdomen. He groaned and stumbled, and shadows deepened in the wound as his blood mingled with the mud.

Lightning flashed and thunder pealed a few seconds later. Hana's blade impaled a warrior, and Mason's blows destroyed the shield of his current opponent. His powerful blow hammered into the Drow's head and the Dark Elf catapulted into a sedan window. His body shattered the glass and shards spewed over him where he sprawled on the vehicle seat.

Alison thrust her blade through the stomach of her enemy while she delivered a staccato rhythm of bolts of bright light magic toward the two Drow nearest Hana. Her friend took advantage of the suppression fire to vault over their adversaries. A few quick stabs were all it took to break through their shields and skewer another assailant. She yanked the *tachi* out in time to twirl and dodge a counter-attack from an unwounded opponent.

Mason grunted as a Drow stabbed through his shield

and into his shoulder. Alison's follow-up light bolt staggered the attacker and allowed the life wizard to launch a series of rapid, enhanced punches. He finished with an elbow strike that depleted the Dark Elf's shield and his final upper-cut hurled his target face-first into the mud.

Another quick attack bounced off the half-Drow's shield with no more than a sting. She replied with a flurry of slices that quickly shredded her latest assailant's shield and scored gaping wounds in his body.

The fox and the bodyguard on either side pressed in with their own attacks. Soon, the additional aggressors fell. Alison finished the battle when she demolished their final opponent's shield with a steady stream of energy bolts that left the woman groaning on the ground, her chest burned.

The Brownstone team hadn't killed any of the Drow, but they were severely wounded. Several stumbled to their feet as the shadows pooled in their wounds to heal them.

Alison summoned another shadow blade and brandished them at Drow. "We've really tried to be nice here. I even told my people not to kill you, but if you want to continue, you will die. Honestly, I don't have a good enough reason to want you dead yet, so give up. Know when you're beaten."

The back door of a sedan opened, and the dark-haired woman stepped out. Her ridiculous heels immediately sank into the muddy ground as a lightning flash revealed a familiar face—Ruby Sumner.

Alison laughed. "Seriously? This is even more twisted than I thought. You hired me to stop you stealing from yourself?"

"I had my reasons, Princess of the Shadow Forged."

Ruby took a few steps forward. Her form blurred, and a beautiful Drow woman in dark, close-fitting, shiny black armor replaced the human. Even though she looked like she was in her twenties by human standards, it was very unlikely that her real age was anywhere close to that.

Shadow wings grew from the Drow's back, and twin shadow blades appeared in her hands. "Your victory was impressive, Princess of the Shadow Forged, but it is as your little many-tailed friend suggested. They never had a chance. I applaud them for their loyalty, and they will be repaid for it. I, on the other hand, am your superior. Submit to me now, or risk death."

CHAPTER TEN

Alison snorted and grew her own shadow wings. "And who the hell are you supposed to be?" It didn't worry her that the Drow was more powerful than her lackeys. All the same principles applied.

Time to engage in another Brownstone family tradition.

The other warriors shuffled behind the new arrival. The healing shadows had almost completely repaired their wounds. The rain continued its ceaseless deluge onto the soft muddy ground, but the lightning and thunder seemed less frequent.

Despite her minor injuries, Alison was clean and dry. Her shields kept the water and mud off her—the blood, too, for that matter.

"I am Rasila," the Drow woman responded, a faint sneer on her face. "And I've put in a lot of effort to meet you, Princess of the Shadow Forged."

She narrowed her eyes and recalled that she'd heard the name a few times during her time on Oriceran. "You're the Princess of the Endless Shadow. Now I know what you've been doing these last few years since you weren't around when I was on Oriceran. Bank accounts and false identities? Using professional middle-men? You know your way around some of the shadier parts of Earth existence. Although you did make the mistake of not creating a back-story for your latest persona."

Mason frowned and Hana gasped.

Rasila gave her a lop-sided smirk. "The gates might still not yet be fully open, but they represent an opportunity. Any Oricerans who ignore Earth consign themselves to weakness and ignorance. I will help lead the Drow into the future, and that requires me to understand Earth as much as Oriceran."

"You set this all up?" She gestured around with her shadow blades. "All this bullshit misdirection?" She pointed one of the tenebrous blades at the SUV. "Is there even anything in the damned box? It's damned light as I recall."

"There's air, I would presume. Or dust." The princess smirked. "But nothing material."

"If you merely wanted to mess with me, why use the box?"

"I was actually curious in several ways. I wanted to know if you would take the assignment, and I wanted to know if you would force the box open once you realized it had Drow magic on it. You're an interesting creature, Alison Brownstone." Her smirk faded and faint hostility entered her eyes. "And I see now it's a mistake to think of you like your adopted father. He's powerful but simpler in many ways. It was worthwhile to perform this experiment."

Alison scoffed. "It's like you said, Hana. It's all some big damned test."

The fox glared at Rasila and harrumphed. "Sometimes, I hate being right."

"A test? Yes, that's an accurate way of putting it." The Drow's now cold gaze swept over Hana and Mason. "Words about your deeds have reached far, even off Earth, Princess of the Shadow Forged. I knew that if I simply approached you and challenged you, the resulting battle would be pointless and useless—not a real reflection of your capabilities—so I concocted this scheme. I needed to give you proper motivation and make you fight like your life was at risk."

She glared at Rasila. "This isn't a damned game. Your people could have been killed. My people could have been killed. You can't simply attack whomever you want, whatever your reasons."

"The risk to your people is irrelevant." She shrugged and a faint look of disbelief colored her face. "As for my people, they weren't permanently harmed. You didn't even kill any when you had the chance. That was another interesting thing I observed."

Alison glanced at the wounded Drow. All of them watched their princess, their faces filled with pride.

Seriously? I fucked you up and you're all happy about it?

"You gambled with their lives," she shouted. "You're supposed to be a princess and protect your people."

"And what of your man and woman?" Rasila nodded at Hana and Mason in turn. "How is their fighting for you any different than my people fighting for me?"

"She fought with us," Mason pointed out. "Skin in the game."

Hana nodded her agreement. "It's easy to hide in a car while everyone else is sliced up."

Rasila sighed wearily. "Your mercy is also well-known, Alison, and you confirmed it. You are perhaps overly merciful, but that doesn't matter because this battle isn't over." She released one of the blades and raised the remaining one, a grin on her face. "We will fight to prove I'm stronger than you."

"No." She snorted derisively. "I'm not here to satisfy your curiosity. At least you paid in advance so this whole thing wasn't a total waste of time. But otherwise, you can screw off back to Oriceran." She turned toward the SUV. "Come on, Hana. Come on, Mason. Let's go."

"You're not leaving," the princess yelled. "Or do you think you can escape me without the lives of your friends being forfeit?"

Alison spun and her face blazed with fury. "Are you serious right now? Did you threaten my friends after all the bullshit you've already thrown at us? You're trying my patience, *princess*."

Rasila studied her speculatively. "If you wish your friends no harm, then you'll fight me to prove your worth as a princess. Our underlings don't need to be involved. There's no risk to them that way, but if you refuse, there are no guarantees. Powerful beings who fight can hurt weaker beings, even when they don't try to—and especially when there's a chaotic melee."

"You have way too much damned nerve, trying to force me to do anything, you bitch."

Her adversary shook her head. "I'm not forcing you. If you truly are a Drow princess, there's no one who could bend you to their will. I'm merely giving you a choice." She drifted a few yards into the air. "But I won't let you hide behind your underlings like a coward."

"Don't do it, A," Mason insisted. "We can take all of them together. Hana and I can keep the rest of them off you. We don't need to play by her rules."

Hana's fingers flexed around the hilt of the *tachi*. "Especially if we go for their heads this time. You can't blame us if they have a death wish."

"No." Alison rose and refreshed her shields. She shook her head. "If she wants to duel princess to princess, that's fine by me. You guys get back to the car. It's about time I made some shit clear to the Drow. This way, no one else gets hurt."

The Brownstone Security team and the remaining Drow backed away from the airborne princesses. Both sides looked uncertain about who might emerge victorious.

"Good," Rasila declared. "This won't be a waste of my time either. I was afraid I would test you and find that my servants were enough to handle you."

"I'm more than enough for them, and more than enough for you."

The Drow princess thrust forward, her shadow blade raised. Alison launched upward and fired a bright bolt. Her opponent didn't even flinch when the attack struck the dark nimbus that surrounded her. Instead, she thrust her open palm out and conjured a spear so dark it was almost invisible in the rain. Alison hissed as the attack struck her.

Her shield helped but didn't block all the energy of the attack.

This isn't too bad so far.

She continued to climb into the windy air as her adversary flung spear after spear at her. Quick spins and twists saved her from several of the shadow projectiles but not all. Her shield spell didn't fail, but pain suffused her body from a few minor wounds.

Okay, she's upped her game. I need to do the same.

Without warning, she careened toward Rasila, launched a series of light blasts, and raised her blade so it pointed directly at the Drow. The princess took several blows and her face twitched before she rolled out of the path of the magic. Alison hurtled past her, but the hasty slash of her blade only weakened her target's shield.

Both women circled one another and traded rapid magical attacks, but the wind made it harder to deliver effective strikes. The half-Drow alternated between bright bolts of light magic and dark, sharp crescents of pure shadow magic. Her challenger replied with shadow spears and orbs that exploded in a barrage of purple-black missiles.

Blood seeped through Alison's shirt, but the pain was easy to ignore.

Burns and holes pitted Rasila's armor and body. A thin line of blood trailed from a head injury that creeping shadows already sealed. Her grin grew wider with each wound.

Alison closed her eyes and hurled a quick flare spell. Her adversary hissed and released her wings to drop toward the ground. The half-Drow pursued the blinded

Princess of the Endless Shadow and channeled more magic into her blade.

The weapon pierced Rasila as she landed, and she winced in pain and tumbled backward. Her deep shoulder wound trailed droplets of blood before she crashed into the hood of one of the sedans with a deep, reverberating thud.

As Alison landed, she let her wings and sword dissipate and thrust her hands forward to force energy into a massive light magic lance. The weapon sailed toward its target and only narrowly missed the wounded woman, who flipped with the aid of a quick air burst spell. The lance drilled into the car to leave a smoldering hole from the front and all the way out the back.

Rasila finished her evasion maneuver when she landed atop the damaged vehicle. A euphoric smile spread over her face as she raised her hands. Instinctively, Alison called her sword once more. Dark, inky tentacles extended from the mud and snapped at her.

Without hesitation, she sliced through them with her shadow blade before she thrust back with a burst spell of her own. She released the force that supported her blade and channeled magical energy into a crackling and rapidly-growing bright white orb between her hands.

It's time to end this. She seems like she's near my level, which means she could take it. Otherwise, we can sit here all day and trade hits.

"Yes!" Rasila shouted from the top of the car. "Show me your true power, Alison. Convince me you're a Drow princess and not some feeble human who knows a few shadow magic tricks." She raised her arms in challenge.

Shadows swirled and danced over them, writhing as if they were alive as they flowed into a glowing and lengthening purple-black lance.

The other Drow continued their retreat from the car, the concern on their faces obvious. Mason and Hana remained near the SUV.

Lightning flashed again in the distance and highlighted the blood- and mud-stained battlefield scored with footprints. Both princesses continued to feed their spells and the powerful magic that radiated from them made the hair on the back of Alison's neck stand up.

If I don't make this stand now, some other princess will show up and it'll be the same bullshit.

Wind-driven curtains of rain fed the growing puddles in the area.

She gritted her teeth and continued to thrust more energy into her hungry spell. Rasila stared with rapt expectation, her face a mask of ecstasy as her own shadow lance grew.

Shit. If I put much more of this in, I might kill her, but I have to make my point. A few more seconds should do it. I need to make sure she never tries this again, and that means she needs to understand that she's outclassed.

Alison yelled defiance as she released the crackling orb, now the size of a basketball. Her adversary responded with a shout of triumph and dropped her arms. Her car-length concentration of shadow energy roared into a headlong assault against the half-Drow.

The blinding white orb met the juddering purple-black lance. A massive explosion enveloped the area and produced a spreading dome of white-purple energy.

The shockwave scattered the Drow like bowling pins and launched both combatants into the air. The dueling princesses tumbled, battered and burned.

Two trees groaned and toppled with a loud crash. Fire dotted several of the other trees nearby, but the heavy rain doused it almost immediately.

Alison hissed in pain as she impacted the unforgiving soil and rolled. Mud coated her now that her shield had deactivated. She dragged in a deep breath and shoved to her feet. The Drow sedans were burned husks of half-melted metal and plastic, mere skeletons of the vehicles they had once been, and one now lay upside down. Something warm fell out of her ear and she scowled when she realized it was her burned receiver.

"Shit. We overdid it a little." She glanced over her shoulder as her stomach knotted.

The Brownstone SUV remained untouched, as did Hana and Mason, although a few smoldering branches decorated the trees near the vehicle.

The fox gave her a thumb's up, her bright tails a beacon in the dark rain. Mason shook his head, but she was too far away to make out his expression.

I know you think that was a dumb move, but I had to do it.

Alison stomped toward the fallen Rasila, who lay—her garments smoking in places—on her back in a shallow puddle several yards away. Her chest still rose and fell. Her warriors sat and winced in pain, heavily burned. Shadows pooled around them again as their magic did its part to restore them.

A few final heavy, splashing steps brought her to her adversary. She extended a shadow blade and put it to the woman's neck. "Don't make me kill you, Rasila. We don't have to be enemies. Surrender already. I won't make you do a silly dance or kiss my feet or anything. You did your tests. Haven't I proven myself? I'm still standing with my weapon to your throat."

She took a few deep breaths and wished she could cast a few healing spells of her own, but she couldn't risk giving the other woman an opening.

Rasila raised her palms, a huge smile on her face despite the burns on her body. "I, Rasila, Princess of the Endless Shadow, yield to Alison Brownstone, Princess of the Shadow Forged."

CHAPTER ELEVEN

"I accept your surrender." Alison backed away slowly, her eyes locked on her opponent. As much as the Drow prized strength, defeating an enemy was an honor of its own, regardless of the method. The use of so many assassins by Laena had only proven that, and it would take a long time and a lot more Drow like Myna for that to change.

They might not be evil, but they also weren't good by typical human standards. Even if Alison was only half-human, she followed those standards, exactly as her non-human adopted father did.

Is it finally over?

Rasila stood slowly, her wounds shrouded with thick shadows. Splatters of red blood marred her white hair. "I'm surprised, Alison." The words came out with a lack of any hint of condescension or smugness. "Very surprised."

"You're surprised about what?" She took the opportunity to retrieve a healing potion from her pocket and drank it quickly. The potion's magic would be more thorough and work faster than if she used her own healing spells. For all her power, she still had a few Drow tricks she needed to improve on, including using shadow magic to recover.

Healing helped, but it wouldn't save her if she didn't try to restrain herself the next time. As long as she kept the princess talking, there would be less risk of a sneak attack—even though she was likely serious about her surrender after the massive explosion.

Rasila raised a white eyebrow and her gaze lingered on the potion before Alison slipped the empty container in her pocket. "Yes, I'm surprised. You're a child by Drow standards. Even with your royal blood, the small number of years of training you received should have not granted you the power you needed to defeat me in battle. I will be honest, I expected to defeat you easily. It's rare that I encounter other Drow who can provide me with such a challenge."

"That's the thing." Alison smiled as the pain of her wounds faded. "You all constantly talk about how human I am, and that's true, but it also means I have access to a mixture of magic and power that you don't. Maybe I've come into my power quicker because of that, too, or maybe it's because of who my adoptive parents are." Her gaze cut to the other Drow. None looked like they were ready to attack her. They all simply looked tired. She knew the feeling.

They were lucky they weren't seriously injured in that final explosion.

"It doesn't matter, I suppose," Rasila replied. "It only matters that you have power, and you've proven it to me in such a way that I can no longer doubt you." She gestured to one of the wrecks. "And it's obvious to me you could accomplish even more destruction if you so desired it. Your defeat of my people proved you were merely competent, but your defeat of me proves that you're dangerous and a threat to a fully trained Drow royal, which makes you a danger to many beings on Oriceran."

She sighed. "Just to be clear, is the test over? I was serious before. I can and do kill people, but I'd rather not kill someone in a duel. I'm not your enemy. The only Drow I've ever had a problem with were Laena and the assassins she sent to Earth, and that's because they targeted me and my family."

The woman threw up a dismissive hand. "It's fine. You have proven yourself to my satisfaction. Fighting another princess to the death would be…inappropriate, even in these barbarous times." Her nostrils flared. "It would have been my fault if I died. I challenged you without a full appreciation of your strength, even though I was aware of your reputation. I admit that I thought some of it might have reflected the human fondness for exaggeration. That was indeed foolishness on my part."

Alison nodded. She wasn't too tired to be annoyed, but at least there wouldn't be a round three and no one had been killed. The locals probably wouldn't appreciate the collapsed trees, but she could make an anonymous donation to cover those.

"Why all this?" She gestured around the blasted area. "If this isn't about killing me or revenge for Laena, what was the point?"

"To test you." Rasila sounded and looked confused. "I thought I was already clear on that."

"I get that. But why here and why now? Why not on Oriceran when I visited? Or before?"

Something approaching disappointment settled onto the Drow's face. "Do you support the Guardians?"

She shrugged. "I'm neutral when it comes to Drow governmental matters. I don't truly understand enough about the culture and history to argue whether it's better to have the Guardians or select a new queen. I know I don't support Laena. She tried to kill my dad and wanted to kidnap me. I wasn't exactly sad when he went after her, and if I had the chance, I would have done so myself."

"Laena was defeated," Rasila replied. "She is no longer relevant, and I will not defend her actions against you and your adopted father. If Laena had been wise, she would have approached you without tricks and attempted to persuade you to visit. But she is the past." She sniffed disdainfully. "And I am concerned about both the past and the future. Queens have led the Drow for thousands of years. I don't care about other types of leaders let alone the laughable method your adopted land uses to select your rulers. The Drow need a queen, and they need a queen soon before our people lose their way. The Guardians don't understand this, even if they claim they do."

"So you are a royalist, then? Your people's smack talk earlier wasn't all part of the test?" Alison frowned, uncertain of where this whole conversation might go. "I'm not saying I support the Guardians, but why are you so certain that they're wrong?"

"You make it sound like a choice, but it's a simple

acknowledgment of what it means to be a Drow." Rasila shrugged. "We can't go against our true nature. The weight of millennia bears down on our people and demands a new queen, not a council of so-called Guardians who aren't even royals." Her face contorted in anger. "And they are nothing but cowardly opportunists. If they wanted to depose Laena, they should have done it themselves and not relied on an outsider. James Brownstone isn't even Oriceran. That failure alone means they don't deserve to rule the Drow."

Alison sighed. "I was only curious. Like I said, I'm neutral. I'm only involved now because you chose to set me up and attack me."

The Drow shook her head. "But the current situation is unstable and untenable, and the time of a new queen will come soon. And that means one of the princesses will need to consolidate power and earn the loyalty of the others—including you, the Princess of the Shadow Forged. That's what it means to hold that title."

"It's not my problem," she declared firmly. "I don't want to be queen. Not even in the slightest. I made that clear during my time on Oriceran, and I've made it clear to every Drow who has asked me or who has said I should be queen. I will not try to disrupt Drow society any more than it already is."

"With your strength and proven deeds, it's a possibility." Rasila shook her head. "Are you so sure you have no interest? For a woman who takes such pride in her great deeds, you demonstrate a curious lack of ambition."

"Yes. I'm not interested in power. I'm interested in protecting people." Alison laughed. "You said I'm a child, and you're not wrong, by your standards. Given how old my mother was, you're probably hundreds of years old. My magic is powerful, but there's a lot I need to learn about myself, let alone Oriceran and Drow society."

"I'm far older than you, yes." Her lop-sided smirk was oddly attractive. "You're wise to realize that."

"And you want a child to lead the Drow?" She shrugged. "A child who grew up thinking she was human? That doesn't make a lot of sense to me, no matter how much ass I can kick."

"Strength can form its own wisdom, and even inexperienced rulers can have advisors. A strong queen is important for the Drow. The rest can be taught."

Alison snorted. "In other words, you want me to be queen while other people pull my strings and I take all the blame. I'm not interested, and I don't know how many times I have to say it before you believe me." She brushed some wet hair out of her eyes.

The rain had lessened, but dark clouds remained.

Rasila raised her chin and squared her shoulders. The shadows that had covered her body faded to leave unmarred flesh visible through the holes in the fabric. "That's true, but if your strength is not used to take the throne, it can be used to support it. You should pledge your support to me, Princess of the Shadow Forged. I have the wisdom and experience to lead our people. With our power combined, the other princesses will fall in line."

She shook her head. "I don't know you well enough, and I don't want to be involved in Drow politics. For all I know, you're a dangerous fanatic planning something stupid and short-sighted. I can't risk screwing over the Drow."

"I see. I can understand your position, even though I don't agree." Rasila stared at her. The rushing wind filled the tense silence between them.

Alison shrugged at last. She needed this to be over. "The best thing I could do for the Drow is to stay out of their business. I'm a disruptive element, and if you truly want things to calm down, it's a terrible idea to involve me. I don't have to be an expert on politics to know it'll probably end with someone declaring that my claim to my title is illegitimate."

"That might not be the case, but it does carry certain responsibilities. The Shadow Forged are the keepers of the wish, and even though you've expended yours, you're not necessarily guaranteed a new one for your future daughter. If you truly intend to keep yourself separate from your people, perhaps the wish line should be transferred. That is something a new queen has the potential to decide."

Her jaw tightened. "Are you trying to threaten me into supporting you? Because I don't take kindly to threats, and I've already proven that I can defend myself."

Rasila raised her hands in a placating manner. "I'm simply voicing possibilities. If you make a decision—even if that decision is to stay neutral—you should be aware of all the implications. Being neutral isn't without potential consequence."

"Fair enough, and it changes nothing." Alison flicked some mud impatiently off her face. "This is one race for the throne that I don't want any part of."

Now mostly healed, the other Drow crept around the

burned wreckages of the vehicle. She might have felt worse for their predicament, but they were at the edge of town, so it wasn't like they were stranded. Their shape-shifting would even save them the trouble of standing out.

The Drow princess shook her head. "It'll be interesting to see how long you can maintain your neutrality. I think you're naïve, perhaps because you're young and too human in how you think, but only time will force you to confront the harsh truth."

Alison snorted. "How long can I maintain my neutrality? How about forever? Or at the minimum, until I die, which might be a few hundred years."

Rasila laughed. "I might be the only princess with the courage and experience to challenge you so directly on Earth, but you can't avoid the succession forever, Alison. Your royal heritage means you're involved, whether or not you want to be. In the future, more will come to challenge you. If not the princesses, then their servants. You're too powerful a contender to be left alone. You represent a threat, and since you refuse to name a side, everyone will assume you're a danger to theirs."

"Then I'll prove to anyone else who shows up why they should leave me the hell alone." She pointed at one of the burned husks that used to be a car. "If I have to do it one by one, eventually, you'll all get the point. That strategy works for my dad, and it also works for me. Do you want a Drow princess threat? All my enemies are either in prison or dead, and the last major enemy I care about will soon be one of those."

I don't have time to mess around with the Drow when the Seventh Order is still out there.

Rasila turned and walked toward her people. "Consider what I've said, Princess of the Shadow Forged. When the time comes, you might find it to your advantage to support me. You may dislike me, but my values, I suspect, are closer to yours than some of the other princesses. I respected Laena's strength, but I thought she was a twisted monster."

"But you never tried to take her down."

She stopped and narrowed her eyes. "I didn't at that. You do make a good point. Perhaps I'm more of a coward than I realized." She continued her retreat.

Alison shook her head and jogged toward the SUV, grateful that her friends had stayed well away from the fight.

Hana sheathed her sword and her tails disappeared. "I couldn't hear most of what she said. Is everything okay? It looks like they're leaving."

"The fight's over if that's what you mean." She took a deep breath and exhaled slowly. "I wish that was the end of my problems with the Drow, though."

Mason frowned. "Will it start again tomorrow?"

"Nothing like that, at least not from that group." She offered her teammates an apologetic smile. "I'll explain in the car. The short version is that it's a bunch of political crap, but it's all over for now."

The wizard glared at the figures retreating into the rain in the distance. "At least they didn't stiff us on the bill." He trudged through the mud to the driver's side. "Next time, maybe we don't step directly into the trap."

The women laughed.

"Maybe," Alison replied. "For now, let's go home."

CHAPTER TWELVE

Tahir shook his head in disgust as he slapped his keycard against the front door lock. It clicked open, and he entered his living room, still in disbelief that Hana had insisted he check on the dog since the job was over.

The animal is in a pen with food and water. What does she think it will do? Blow itself up?

The puppy lay on a pillow in the small enclosure. He bounded to his feet as the infomancer entered, barked, and wagged his tail before he ran a few times in a circle.

His reluctant caregiver wandered closer and frowned. "As I thought, plenty of food and water." He glanced at the clean paper that lined the floor of the pen. "And you've not even made a mess. I'll grant you that. Did you wait?" He shook his head. "But why can we sense magic? What are you hiding, dog?"

He turned away from the happy puppy and headed toward his refrigerator. The dog barked once more and panted.

"I want some juice. You'll survive with your water, dog."

He located it in the fridge and poured himself a cup. "If you live with us, you'll need to learn that not all things are for animals. That's a matter of health for you and simple dignity for me and Hana."

Half the juice was gone when he sensed a pulse of magic from behind him. He frowned and turned slowly, half-expecting a Drow assassin, but there was no one there.

I know I felt something, but what? My wards would have activated if someone portaled or broke in.

A soft meow filled the air.

Tahir lowered his gaze apprehensively to the pen as a frown built between his eyes. A small brown kitten stood where the puppy had been moments before and stared at him with precious little eyes.

"Oh, I see," he muttered. He retrieved his phone from his pocket and dialed Hana.

"What's up, babe?" She answered almost on the first ring. "Is my adorable puppy all right? He still has water, right?"

"He's...all right," he answered carefully. "And his supplies are well-maintained."

She laughed. "What's wrong? You sound concerned. Wait. Is he sick?"

The infomancer stared at the furball. He knew it was the same animal—aside from the fact that he'd seen it with his own eyes before the weird transformation, he wore the same collar Hana had purchased for him the night before. "I discovered why we've sensed magic from the animal. He demonstrated a magical ability."

"Oh!" Hana shouted over the line. "He can teleport, can't he? We'll play some awesome games of fetch. This is why magical pets rock. I would have preferred a dragon, but this is almost as good, and it's not like I'd be able to fit a dragon in our place."

Tahir sighed. "No, he can't teleport, but he also might not be a dog. I'm fairly certain he's not a dog—at least not all the time."

"So he's a dog-like being?" she ventured nervously. "There are many of those out there. No big deal."

"What I mean is that he's a cat now," he explained and narrowed his eyes on the cute brown kitten.

"A cat?" She sounded confused. "What? Did he knock over a glass or something? Dogs do that kind of thing, too, you know. Not all of them are these brave, howling hunters."

The infomancer sighed. "No, you don't understand. He's literally a cat—as in he's changed shape. He's the same color and about the same size, but he's now a cat instead of a dog. I sensed a major pulse of magic before he did it."

Hana squealed in excitement. "Are you kidding me? If you're messing with me, you won't get any for a month."

"I'm telling you the truth." He groaned. "You know I'm not one for practical jokes and other such forms of unnecessary humor. Your pet is a shapeshifter of some sort."

"Perfect. Absolutely perfect!" Scratching rasped over the line, and Hana said something he couldn't make out. He presumed she was explaining the situation to Alison and Mason.

He continued to stare at the cat, the phone against his ear, and waited for the surprisingly long alternate conversation to finish.

You don't seem like an intelligent being, but you could be hiding that, too.

"Do you know what this means?" Hana asked eventually.

"I can think of many possibilities, but why don't you explain what you think it means to you?"

Tahir loved Hana and her thirst for life, but he'd long since learned that her mind didn't always follow the most rational path. The best strategy, sometimes, was to simply ask rather than try to anticipate the chaotic fox's intentions. He'd learned that was definitely easier than to try his analytical approach, only to be frustrated.

"It's not simply any pet, babe," she clarified.

He snorted. "We already knew that. We simply now understand the specific nature of the magic."

"No, no, no. You don't get it. It's not simply any pet. It's maybe all cute pets in one! If he's a cat now, maybe he'll be a bird tomorrow and then a lizard. I'll never get bored with him because he'll cycle through things. He's the ultimate pet."

"You can't be sure of that." He managed to resist yet another sigh. "It might very well be that he only alternates between cat and dog form. I wouldn't get your hopes up."

The fox laughed. "Listen to you. 'Only alternates between cat and dog form.' He's still way more awesome than any normal dog or cat, even if that's true."

"I suppose, but this kind of creature is undoubtedly highly illegal as well. There are no such pets available at reputable breeders and stores."

She blew a raspberry. "So what? How many technically illegal things do you do each day? I have a long list of felonies I've committed. I think keeping a cute animal is fairly low on the list."

Tahir pinched the bridge of his nose. "I won't dispute that, but I have to remind you that you won't be able to show this pet off to random strangers unless you want to risk attracting the attention of the authorities."

"Screw random strangers. This is my special pet. I knew that if I waited long enough, I'd get something cool."

He rolled his eyes, thankful that this wasn't a face to face conversation. She'd been half-ready to buy everything in the pet store the last few times she'd visited. "There will be difficulties. If he changes forms, he might change into other species and you'll need more than only the pen. A birdcage, for example, or an aquarium. Are you prepared for that?"

"Nope, but it sounds fun. Let's buy some of that stuff tomorrow. Maybe something in case he turns into a cute little lizard, too."

He sighed in defeat. "I'll rearrange some furniture tonight."

Hana curled on the couch and smiled at the purring kitten in her arms. "There's no way I'll give him away now. I don't care if the Fixer himself shows up and claims him."

Tahir shrugged uncomfortably in his chair. "I've removed all the missing pet ads and inquiries I had out and directed my efforts to erase them from the net. If he is some kind of illegally smuggled Oriceran animal or magical experiment, the last thing we want is an open line of evidence that leads directly here."

"Since we're keeping him, we need a name." She frowned a little in concentration. "But it can't be a name that only fits one type of animal. It has to work for him regardless of what form he's in, and it has to be cute and adorable, exactly like him."

"I wouldn't begin to have an idea," her boyfriend replied stiffly. "I'm not good at naming things."

"Mr. Everything?" Hana suggested and held the cat up to study him. "No, that sounds like some weird super-hero, and it's not cute at all." She nuzzled the kitten's nose, and he meowed. "Supercutey?"

He scoffed. "Isn't that a little on-the-nose?"

"At least I'm trying. Why don't you give me some suggestions?"

The infomancer did his best to look interested as he rubbed his chin and cycled through different possibilities in his mind. He decided on some vague level that naming was a mental exercise in the end, and he should be able to apply his vast intelligence to the problem to solve it.

"Omni," he declared after a few seconds.

"Omni?" She frowned. "It's not cute."

"It accurately captures his nature, and it has no hard consonants." He gestured toward the cat. "It's similar to short names associated with many people's animals."

Hana set the cat back into her lap. "What do you think, boy? Do you want to be called Omni?"

The kitten meowed loudly.

"Omni, it is." She grinned. "Are you sure you have no idea how to make him change?"

Tahir shook his head firmly. "I didn't see it until afterward, so I have no idea what might have precipitated the transformation."

She stroked the furry head. "Do you think there's a trigger? It's not simply a time thing?"

"I have no basis on which to provide even a remote guess with regard to how this mystery animal's powers function," he replied flatly. "For all I know, he might change every time a certain musical instrument is played." He took a breath and his face softened. "We probably can't risk taking him to the Brownstone Security building. Even if he's well-trained and in control, if he changes in front of the wrong person and they report it, the government might come and take him, and it might cause trouble for Alison."

The fox sighed. "I know. It sucks that I won't be able to show Omni off to everyone, but we can bring Sonya, Alison, and Mason over." Her face brightened. "But in the meantime, I'll have a great time trying to work out how he changes."

Myna folded her hands behind her back as she stared at Elliot Bay through the living room window. "You know she's right, my princess."

Alison groaned from the couch. She had explained what happened with Rasila and had hoped—foolishly—for a different response. "I knew the minute I called you that you would say something like that."

The old Drow turned from the window, a hint of a

smile on her face. "I offer you what I always offer—loyalty and truth. The Princess of the Endless Shadow can be reasonable, provided her desire for battle is sated, but everything she told you about others coming is correct. There is one small benefit to what happened, though."

"What's that? Knowing that I can take on another Drow princess?"

Her mentor shook her head. "That's useful knowledge as well, but not what I suggested. Rasila is known for her lack of tact and restraint."

"Meaning what? Other than that she was willing to ambush me after she hired me to carry an empty box."

"It's not surprising that she came at you first and in such a blatant and violent manner." Myna walked to the couch and her huge skirt swished with each step. She sat before responding. "And when she returns to Oriceran, she will make it publicly known that she engaged the Princess of the Shadow Forged in a battle, even if it angers the Guardians. It'll spread easily because of who she is."

Alison scoffed. "Good. Maybe that'll keep her off my ass, for a while at least."

"It will, and it will also likely prevent the other princesses from launching any immediate attacks or schemes against you. They'll assume you'll be more prepared for an incident. That's useful, but it'll only delay things."

"Rasila acted like actually killing another princess is something they frown on," she replied. "So it's not like I have to worry about assassination attempts, right?"

Myna nodded. "That's true. The struggle for the throne won't be a series of assassination attempts. Such viciousness is supposed to be reserved for the queen, and any chance of becoming queen will vanish if they go out of their way to break more customs than have already been violated. She'll be viewed, I suspect, as nothing more than a new Laena, and the factions will unite against her."

"But I'll have to deal with my tests, though?"

"Perhaps, or other princesses will approach you directly to establish an alliance, much like Rasila desired."

"When?" Alison asked.

"Not anytime soon, I don't think," the old Drow mused thoughtfully. "This situation has become critical, but we're still talking about Drow time, not human time."

She allowed herself a sigh of relief. "Maybe months then?"

Her companion responded with a slight nod. "Most likely. I wouldn't think it would take years, though."

"Fine. I can work with months. I have way too much on my plate right now anyway, because I really believe the dark wizard confrontation will come in weeks, not months."

CHAPTER THIRTEEN

Izzie crested the concrete stairs and marched resolutely to a line of worn wooden doors. Her contact's apartment was the first. She glanced to her side over a concrete barrier and into the bright lights of London at night.

Liverpool. London. Paris. Everything simply runs together.

Her travels had taken her all over the world. The reach of the dark wizards and the Seventh Order extended that far. While sometimes, every city seemed a variation of the same themes, small details—like the slowly rotating London Eye Ferris wheel in the distance—reminded her that every place was unique and special, even if she didn't always pay attention to those things.

I don't even appreciate the places I go to. Instead, I locate the contacts or bounties, stay a few days, and leave. What good was it to get my memories back if I can't make any new ones?

She snorted and shook her head as she reminded herself that she was damned close to ending the threat now. The victory was so close she could taste it. All she needed was a few final pieces of information, and the wizard behind the closed door would be the start of that.

The bounty hunter raised her hand, knocked three times, and waited. Reclaiming her life had been hard, but between her friends and her parents, the pieces were ready to be glued together.

A few seconds later, the electronic lock clicked, and the door creaked open.

A single suspicious brown eye peeked out. "How do I know it's really you?" demanded a tired English voice as creaky as the door. "It could be them and this is a trick. It's not like you told me exactly when you would come, and you also said you wouldn't be here for a month."

Lies to contacts, as rude as they were, helped to reduce unfortunate encounters. She had learned that over the years.

Izzie scoffed. "Because if I were them, they wouldn't bother to pretend to be me, Nigel. I didn't decide to travel from Liverpool to London because I felt like it. I found important info there, and now, I'm following up on that with you. So, let me in, and let's talk."

Nigel sighed and opened the door. The tired-looking, white-haired old man stood with his hand on an ornate black cane. He wore a frayed brown sweater and nodded toward a ripped tan couch in the center of the tiny living room. Several wet shirts were draped over the back.

She stepped inside and he closed the door behind her.

The bounty hunter raised her hands and chanted a quick spell.

Her host limped over to the couch. "Oy, I should have ignored your letter. I don't even know how you got the information you called me about. This is nothing but a bloody pain for me. That's why I threw my wand into the Thames."

Faint magic clung to the room, and more than a few glyphs nestled in corners if one knew where to look. She suspected that the old wizard hadn't fled as far from his old life as he claimed, even if dark wizards had sent him into a fearful retirement.

"It doesn't matter where I got the information," she explained. "The point is that I have it, and I know you have something I need—something that will help me track and eliminate them." She narrowed her eyes as he sat and rested his hands atop his cane. "You shouldn't want to protect them. You're lucky they haven't killed you already." She gestured around the room. "They're the reason you have to hide in a tiny little flat and not live your life. You admitted to me in the past that you made mistakes helping them, but you never told me you knew the name of one of their leaders."

Nigel's laugh was bitter. "You can't stop the Seventh Order. You're one woman, Berens. Yes, you're a bloody brilliant fighter, but they have an army of wizards. And they won't kill me anytime soon if I keep my bloody mouth shut. They think they're better than that. You always have to remember that in their world, you're the villain, and they're the saviors of Earth."

Izzie scoffed. "And how are you so sure that they won't kill you? These people don't care about hurting innocent people, so why would they allow someone like you to continue to live? You're a threat to them. A threat to saving Earth, from their perspective, as you yourself pointed out."

The wizard patted his knee. "Because the leaders like knowing that people who have failed suffer. They let me know that they're still watching on occasion. I'll go to a store or a pub, and someone from the old days will bump into me and casually ask me about my knee." He shook his head. "They know I don't use the right kind of magic to live longer. I suspect the bloody bastards want to see me fall apart and die from nature's touch."

"Doesn't that piss you off?" She folded her arms. "If I'd been crippled by a curse and tortured, I'd want some payback, whether or not I used to believe in their cause."

He shook his head. "I'm not strong enough for revenge. This way, I give them no excuse to target my daughter. Without magic, she'll always be at risk from them."

"Why agree to help me at all, then? It seems like the order took your balls when they cursed you." She dropped her arms and her hands curled into fists. "Or do you still believe in them?"

"No. I stopped believing in them years ago." He stared at his gnarled hands. "I saw too many things, too many wasted lives."

"Then why?"

Nigel sighed and met her gaze. "Because you saved my daughter that one time when she was caught up in that mess. Without you..." He slumped on his couch and released a long sigh. "And I like to convince myself that maybe she'll be safe if somehow, the Seventh Order is destroyed, but that's mad. I know that, but I can't help but hope."

"Is it really so impossible?" Izzie asked. "They aren't gods or immortals, only a bunch of asshole wizards and witches with superiority complexes. That doesn't even make them unique."

"But they have money, power, and an army," he countered.

She shrugged. "They might have an army, but I have friends of my own whom I can bring to the party once I identify all the appropriate targets." She ticked off a finger. "Conrad Barnes." She ticked off another finger. "Tabitha Nelson. That's two, thanks to my nice little trip up north recently that confirmed that piece of information. I know there are four leaders in the Seventh Order. They aren't safe if I can find this out. You can help. I know you can. Your name came up in Liverpool."

The old man swallowed awkwardly. "If you stopped fighting back, stopped hunting them, you could settle down somewhere and live a normal life. Like they let me and my daughter do. They're ruthless, but they see themselves as aristocracy. You simply have to acknowledge their authority."

"They're hunting me." She shook her head. "And my mother. And I doubt it'll end with them patting me on the head and sending me home. There's no way I could ever settle down, and it doesn't matter. They've taken so much from me already." She stared at her companion. "It's like I said in the letter. I know you have information for me, and you should be able to understand from what I just explained why I won't give up and why I will defeat them. So give it up and I'll go on my merry way."

"If they found out I told you, they would kill me, and they would torture me more first. You know they would."

Izzie stormed close to him. "So, what, you'll sit in this

room and rot? You'll hope they never torment you again? Or they don't decide your daughter is a liability?"

Nigel tensed and licked his lips. "You can't stop them. No one can. They're too careful."

"Too careful? I know half their leadership, and their big plans in places like Seattle have been stopped." She leaned forward, her expression dark as she loomed over the old wizard. "So tell me what I know you already know. The fact that I even sent you that letter and said I'd come should have let you know that I've made progress. Every name I learn makes it that much easier. You have a choice. Either you can sit here and be afraid, or you could help me and take your life back."

"It's too late," he whispered. "But it's Jeanne Martin. That's what you want, isn't it? She's another Seventh Order leader unless they've changed." He shrugged.

"Jeanne Martin?" She shook her head. "See, it's not too late. Not if you really want to fight back. You can defeat the order and reverse the curse. You can actually spend time with your daughter." She looked around. "I'm surprised you've let her out of your sight if you're so paranoid."

"You don't understand." Tears welled in his eyes.

Oh, shit.

She tensed and backed toward the front door. "What have you done?"

"I had no choice. They came a few weeks ago. They know you helped me in the past. They told me that if you ever came, to activate the spell to call them." He pointed toward the front door.

Izzie spun and her heart thumped painfully in her chest. A small glyph glowed near the side of the door. She'd not noticed it in the light but pervasive background magic of the room.

Damn it. I was so thirsty for info, I let my guard down.

Nigel sighed. "If you want to kill me, I understand, but I had to do it. They have my daughter. They said they would give her back if I contacted them and distracted you long enough for them to arrive."

"Where is she right now?" Izzie asked.

"What difference does it make?"

"Because I'll rescue her and stash her somewhere safe. She'll have to hide—not for years like me, but at least she'll have a chance until I defeat the Seventh Order."

A ghost of hope appeared in his eyes and he rattled off an address. "That's where they were last." He pointed toward his closed bedroom door. "You can go out the window in the back. I'll talk to them when they come and try to give you some time. If you go right away, I can make sure they're not ready for you. I deserve to rot, but my daughter doesn't. I'll never be able to defeat them, but you...you might have a chance."

"I'll save her. You have my word." She nodded and rushed to the bedroom, where she threw the door open and hurried to the window. After layering a shield over her body, she shoved the window open and crawled out. She was several stories up but that was the least of her present worries.

The bounty hunter leapt out and muttered a hasty spell to cushion her rapid fall to the hard-packed, grass-covered earth. She landed with a small jolt as if she'd merely jumped from a first-story window.

Izzie looked over her shoulder and shook her head. She

had the information she needed to both save Nigel's daughter Charity and continue her investigation.

A light jog took her several blocks away from the council estate building to a rental car parked farther up the street.

They'll realize what he's done and torture it out of him. I'll have to move on Charity right away if I want any chance to save her.

She whirled at the loud boom of an explosion behind her.

Smoke poured from the side of the building, the wizard's apartment the source.

"Okay, Nigel, you did your part. It's time for me to do mine."

CHAPTER FOURTEEN

Izzie launched upward and her spell gave her height an Olympian could only dream of. She landed on the next roof and ran to the edge before she leapt to another flat one nearby. Several deep breaths as she slowed eased her heart rate a little, and she walked across the almost level surface on top of the three-story building toward a door in the center.

The Seventh Order can tell all the fairy tales they want about being the saviors of the Earth, but they do nothing but leave a trail of corpses. If so many people have to die for their perfect world, you'd think they would finally realize what a fucking ridiculous plan it is.

She drew her pistol and checked it. The problem with wizards was the same as it was for everyone—habit. When a man had a hammer, everything was a nail, and if he had a wand, a spell was the solution to every problem.

"Let's see how careful you bastards actually are."

The bounty hunter raised her hand and cast a quick revelation spell, expecting a dense number of glyphs to appear on the roof door. Even casting her spell risked alerting someone.

She bit back a laugh when nothing appeared. They'd gotten cocky and ignored their roof access point. That made things far easier.

In all honesty, though, she wasn't that surprised. She'd already spotted Charity in the distance with the help of a magnification spell. The light-haired young woman in her early twenties sat at a computer. Even though she looked stiff and upset, anyone from the outside might think she was merely an annoyed employee working overtime.

Is this another trap? Even if it is, I have to get her out of there. I promised I would.

Once she'd layered a new shield over herself, Izzie traced a glyph on the door with her finger and whispered an incantation. The entire door glowed yellow and clicked open.

She pushed into the stairs, her gun in hand, and closed the door quietly behind her. There was only one way to go —down. Light, careful steps took her to the third-floor stairwell.

The bounty hunter breathed deeply and kicked the door open.

The entire room was lined with two long tables that held rows of computers and chairs. Charity sat in front of a computer in the center. Two men lingered near a coffee pot on the other side of the room.

The guards looked up and scrabbled hastily in their jackets for their wands.

Izzie fired three rounds into the first man. He screamed

and fell as she turned and fired at the second, but the bullets simply bounced off.

The wizard scoffed. "This is why I told the bloody fool to keep a shield on him."

She holstered her weapon. "Turn and run right now, and you don't have to die. I'm only here for the woman."

In response, he pointed his wand and chanted a spell. The portion of the table nearest her exploded in a shower of sharp plastic and wooden shards. She grunted, almost blinded, but felt only a light sting because of her shield.

Her instinct pushed her through the cloud of debris. She threw her arm up to cast a quick shield spell over Charity before she launched a fireball at her adversary.

The man hissed and stumbled back as the attack struck him. She pelted him with another fireball and maintained the barrage until he cried out when her final missile burned through his shield and into his chest.

Charity's eyes widened. "Izzie Berens?"

"I keep having to save you." She darted over to her. "Let's go."

The woman's mouth twitched, but she didn't say anything. Instead, she nodded at her arms, which lay on the armrest of the black rolling office chair. Without the wizards to distract her, Izzie could detect the magic over the woman.

She placed her hand on the nearest shoulder and uttered a quick counter-spell.

The captive shivered and rubbed her arms. "I owe you again, Izzie."

"Are those the only two?"

She nodded. "There were more, but they left in a mad

dash." She stood quickly. "I expect they did that to go after you. I wondered why they suddenly paralyzed me with a spell instead of having me sit in the empty office like before."

The bounty hunter gestured to the door. "We'll talk as we run."

Both women sprinted out and down the stairs.

Charity didn't speak again until they reached the first floor. She huffed and puffed between her words. "I knew Dad would find you and you would save me. I never doubted him."

Izzie's expression remained hard and cold as they approached a fire exit. Lying about Charity's father wouldn't lessen the blow when the time came. She deserved to know the truth.

"Your father's dead," she said curtly as she barreled through a fire exit.

The fire alarm screamed.

The woman paled and slowed. "Dead?"

She grabbed Charity's arm and dragged her along. "He blew himself up and took a few of the bastards with him, but the last thing he wanted from me was to rescue you, so I'm here doing exactly that."

This will turn bad. She'll blame me, but I have to get her to trust me long enough to get her somewhere safe.

No tears welled up in the woman's eyes, however, and no sad expression appeared. Instead, her face contorted in burning anger.

"Those bloody bastards," she muttered with her jaw clenched. "They already hurt him so much, and they forced him into that, too?"

"I'm sorry," Izzie replied. "I'm close to eliminating the Seventh Order, but I know that's not much comfort."

Charity took a few deep breaths and pulled her arm free. They continued to run up the street.

"Is there anything I can do?" she asked a few blocks later. "I might not have magic, but you shot one of the wizards. I could shoot one or two or ten. I have to avenge my dad."

The bounty hunter shook her head. "I'll get revenge for both of us. How long were you with them?"

"A few days, why?"

"Did they talk around you at all?" She glanced over her shoulder to confirm that no one had followed them. "I wondered if they mentioned any names. In particular, Conrad, Tabitha, and Jeanne. Anything you might remember that involves those names would be helpful. Those are the people who are ultimately responsible for your father being hurt and killed and you being kidnapped."

The woman's breath caught, and she slowed as recognition dawned on her face. "Conrad, Tabitha, and Jeanne, you said?"

Izzie matched her pace and nodded. "Yes."

"I did hear something on the first day. The bastards were far away, and I couldn't hear much, but one of them said something about Zachariah helping Jeanne...being on her side. It stuck in my mind because Zachariah's such an old-fashioned name." She sighed. "Does that help?"

"Yes, it helps a lot." The grin needed to be pushed back, despite the fact that it wanted out. Looking too happy when Charity had just lost her father would be a bitch move.

"What happens now?" the woman asked as they crossed a street. "I assume I can't go back to our flat."

She shook her head. "That place is a smoking ruin, anyway. I have some money I can give you, and I know someone in town who'll be able to take you somewhere safe until this is all over."

"How long will that be?"

"I hope, based on what you said, not long at all." She looked up as a few drones flew overhead.

The Seventh Order's disinterest in modern technology was one of their greatest strengths and weaknesses simultaneously. Their reduced electronic presence had made them harder to investigate, but relying so much on magic also meant that they didn't always prepare for a technological threat. She had exploited that little fact in the past through the use of things such as EMPs to knock lights out before a raid.

"If my dad made you promise to save me," her companion began tentatively, "I have a different thing to ask."

"Oh?" They turned a corner to where the rental car was parked a little farther down the street. "What? I'm not in the habit of handing wishes out to people."

"Promise me you'll smash the bloody Seventh Order into bits."

The bounty hunter snorted. "That, I can promise."

<hr>

Her hotel bed was surprisingly comfortable. Izzie yawned and stretched. Charity was on her way to a safe house in Ipswich, even though the Seventh Order might not pursue her and simply decide that her usefulness to them was at an end.

The woman had meant nothing but leverage against her father, and he was now dead, another sacrifice to the dark wizards' twisted plans.

She'd told her to lay low for about a month. By then, she assumed it would all be over, one way or another.

"Zachariah, huh?" The bounty hunter tucked her hands under her head as she stared at the ceiling. She needed to take the Starbucks train to Seattle and make contact with Alison. Her friend's infomancers could help to search the world a lot more efficiently than she could manage.

Am I wrong? Even if this Zachariah is the fourth leader of the Seventh Order, they might never meet together.

Izzie frowned as she considered that possibility. While her concern was definitely justified, it didn't negate the enemy's vulnerability. It only meant that she would need help—and not only from Alison. They might have to launch a series of coordinated surprise attacks. Her parents were still away on their own mission, but Alison could bring enough people to help.

If fortune smiled on them, the Seventh Order would all gather in one place. After years of being on the run, she decided she was due a little good luck.

A pulse of magic alerted her a second before the wall exploded. She flung her arms in front of her face as the blast knocked her bed, then cast a shield spell and gritted her teeth before she grimaced and spat out drywall chips.

Damn it. At least I got Charity somewhere safe before anyone tracked me.

A low hum filled the air.

"Surrender, Berens," a man shouted from outside. "No one will come to help you or anyone else here. If you don't immediately surrender, we might have to make an example of the rest of the people staying at this place."

"That would get you too much attention."

"Like Seattle did?" The man clucked his tongue.

"You son of a bitch," she called in response as she stood, her arms up and ready to cast a spell. "You're supposed to be these great noblemen and women leading Earth to a golden age, and you'll kill innocent people?"

A half-dozen dark wizards stood in a line with their wands poised. Their shields glimmered and several wand tips glowed.

A blond man in the middle with a perfect smile nodded. "When you create a beautiful statue, you have to cut away the excess, and that's what we'll do here. Besides, we won't make that choice, you will. And if you think you can win against us, that may well be true. But can you win against us before we can hurt anyone else?"

Izzie's gaze darted from man to man. She took measured, deep breaths but her heart galloped. She might not care about risking her own life, but if she let innocent people get hurt to save herself, she wouldn't be any better than the damned Seventh Order.

Would I have enough time to strengthen the building? I could concentrate on that. My shields should hold long enough, I think, and they aren't here to kill me. They're here to take me back to the order. I can use that.

"This was inevitable, Berens," the wizard shouted. "A single woman can't resist an entire group of dedicated wizards forever."

She took a few steps forward and sighed. A woman peeked through her curtains a couple of rooms down, fear on her face. Shouts sounded from around the corner.

This wasn't an abandoned parking lot or a dark wizard base. There was too much risk of collateral damage.

Izzie drew a deep breath and turned. It was time to test how wide an area she could protect with her powers.

"Surrendering, Berens?" the wizard asked. "Good."

Something exploded behind her. Men screamed in agony and she whirled to see where the assault had come from.

A crater marred the ground where the leader had stood. There wasn't much left of him, and his comrades lay on the ground, groaning and bleeding. A woman in a leather jacket and motorcycle helmet strode toward them. Throwing knives glowed red in her hands.

The wizards hissed in fury and turned toward the woman. The bounty hunter used the opportunity provided by their distraction to fire a blast of concentrated light magic at one of her adversaries. His shield was already depleted from the explosion and offered no protection. He screamed and his body toppled as his shriek cut off. A few more measured strikes eliminated the remainder.

Izzie approached the new arrival cautiously. The woman pulled her helmet off to reveal shoulder-length dark hair with blue streaks and prominent bangs.

"Not the tidiest kill, but it got the job done," she said cheerfully in a Welsh accent and chuckled. "I should have known if I followed the bloody bastards around it would have led to you." She shrugged. "Or Brownstone." She gestured into the distance. "If you don't mind riding behind me, we could leave on my bike."

Something about the woman's appearance seemed familiar—like someone had described her to Izzie before.

Wait. A Welshwoman with that look? From what Alison said, she should be dead.

"Not that I don't appreciate your help, but who the hell are you?" she asked.

The witch grinned. "Drysi Jones."

Fifteen minutes later, the two were parked in a lot outside a shadowed park. A few birds watched them from the trees, but there wasn't anyone or anything else around.

Izzie stepped off the bike and backed away, a frown on her face. This could be another trick. The dark wizards might be arrogant, but their backup plans had steadily improved, especially since her and Alison had disrupted so many of their schemes in recent years.

Drysi dismounted and removed her helmet. She shook her hair out, the gesture casual and relaxed. "This is as good as a place as any to talk, and if anyone does show up to kill us, we don't have to worry about anyone else getting hurt." She grinned. "The elusive Izzie Berens. It's strange to talk to you. I know we're not mates or anything, but I feel like I know you since the Seventh Order has been obsessed with you and your family for so many years."

"You don't know anything about me," Izzie scoffed. "You assholes hunted us like dogs."

The witch propped herself on the edge of her bike's seat and folded her arms. "I'm not saying it's right. I know it's wrong. That's why I'm here. That's why I helped you."

"You helped save a lot of lives back there, but that doesn't mean I trust you," she pointed out. "Even if you did help Alison on that island, and I honestly don't give you any credit for DC since that was merely part of your cover. As far as I'm concerned, you're simply another potential dark wizard trap."

Her companion nodded. "I won't lie, I expected that, and I deserve it, too. You can do a truth spell on me if you want. I have nothing left to hide and no pride left to lose."

The bounty hunter shrugged. "I'll need to pat you down first and make sure you don't have any artifacts that will mess with it. I'm not an idiot. A professional liar like yourself has more than a few tricks."

She studied the woman with narrowed eyes. Low levels of magic radiated off her, but they felt like wards rather than anything else.

"Fair enough." The Welsh witch unzipped her jacket and handed it over. She wore a vest that held a dozen throwing knives and a wand. Izzie took the jacket, dug into the pockets, and searched for artifacts. She found more knives and a couple of healing potions before she handed the jacket back and Drysi hung it from a handlebar. The actual pat-down didn't net any jewelry or artifacts either.

"Satisfied? And you didn't even buy me a drink first." The woman smirked.

"Very funny." She glared at her. "But this isn't a joke to me, and it isn't a joke to all the people the order has killed or hurt."

Drysi scoffed. "What is with all you Americans? Don't you have a sense of humor?" She folded her arms. "It's not a bloody joke to me either. I helped them. I know the kinds of things they do and plan, which is why I'm trying to do something to stop it, even though it'll likely get me killed or worse. But I won't bloody mope about it."

"Do you want a medal for not being an evil bitch for all of five seconds?" Izzie replied with a shrug. "Go ask for one from Alison. She's the one who's obsessed with seeing the good in everyone. Me? I'm the official bitchy friend. Are you ready for the truth spell? If you're lying to me, don't expect to make it out of here alive."

"Do whatever you need to do. For the first time in my life, I'm not hiding anything."

The bounty hunter made a series of intricate motions with her hand as she chanted the spell. She fed magic in carefully at prescribed intervals until a glowing white ball appeared in front of her.

"Are you Rhazdon?" she asked. "Answer yes."

Drysi stared at her like she'd lost her mind. "What?"

"Answer the damned question like I said."

"Yes, I'm Rhazdon, terrible Atlantean scourge." She shook her head, disgust on her face.

The orb turned black.

Izzie nodded, satisfied. "I needed to be sure. Are you ready now?"

"Fine. Go ahead." The woman shrugged but her smile was a little sad.

"Are you Drysi Jones, bounty hunter and former dark witch?"

"I am."

The ball remained white.

"Are you serious about fighting the Seventh Order? Even if it costs you your life?"

"I am."

"Why do you want to fight the Seventh Order?"

Drysi sighed. "Because Alison showed me there's a better way, and the Seventh Order are right bastards who will stab us all in the back even if they get what they want. They said it was all about returning order to the world, but it's a damn lie, and they're monsters. I should have seen and accepted that after the Mountain Strider, but I didn't."

Izzie stared at the ball but it reflected no change, not even a slight shift. She released its energy. "They probably thought you were dead before. If anyone watched that fight, they now know you're alive and that you helped me. You get that, right?"

The witch scoffed. "I have so many counter-tracking wards on both me and my bike that there's no way they can find me. You're not the only one who can hide in the shadows, Berens. Being a sneaky bitch for the last few years means I understand how to hide when I need to." Her shoulders slumped. "But you're right. Everything I know about the order says they want you alive. Me? Once they realize I've betrayed them and that I'm alive, they'll find me and torture me as an example. I should hide in a hole so dark it makes a black hole look bright."

She shook her head, her lip curled in derision. "But I'm tired of doing nothing while people like you and Alison fight them. I need to stop them, and I need to pay them back for everything they've done not only to me but to so many innocent people." She focused her gaze on her palm.

"Especially since some of those innocent people are dead because of me."

The bounty hunter drew a deep breath. "Based on everything I know and what you've said, if I killed you right here, the world might be a better place. Just because you've suddenly decided to not be an awful evil bitch doesn't make you a good person."

"You think I'm an evil bitch? You're right, I am. And I know there's not enough bleach in the two worlds to wash the blood off my hands, but at least I want it to be not quite so thick. But you know what?"

"What?"

Drysi smirked. "You really are the bitchy friend compared to Alison."

She tried not to laugh but it sneaked out anyway. "I can't deny that." She shrugged. "She's always been too sweet for her own good, all the way back to when I first met her. Even all the bounty hunting and dark wizard hunting hasn't changed that. Her agency is full of strays. A questionable infomancer and a former con-woman. She's exactly like her father, obsessed with giving people second chances but acting like she's as tough as nails."

"And you?" The woman's tone wasn't upset or accusatory, more curious. "Are you as merciful?"

"Me? Hell no." Izzie shrugged. "I let the world beat me down more, or maybe I was always harder deep down. I've been on the run a long time, investigating your former friends and all the awful things they do. I've saved people from terrible criminals and seen too many corrupt people get away with shit to be idealistic. I don't even know what

I'll do with myself once I've destroyed the order. More bounty hunting, I guess."

"Alison needs someone like you. Or me." Drysi looked thoughtful. "She really does."

She narrowed her eyes. "Meaning what? She needs more ruthless killers around her?"

"I had a truthbender when I approached her before." The witch blinked and shook her head. "I lost the bloody thing when I ended up in the ocean, but I don't think I ever actually needed it. Alison's very trusting—too trusting. Life's not always tidy, but she seems to think it is. She's always willing to risk herself to help other people when she should ask herself whether that's even worth doing."

"That's because she's been able to save people. She has the power, so I think she feels she has to." Izzie pinched the bridge of her nose. "But what does that have to do with either you or me? Why does she need someone like us around her?"

"Don't you see? If she always sees the good in people, she needs someone who always sees the bad. That way, dark witches won't get near her and have a good chance to assassinate her." Drysi grinned but it faded a few seconds later into a scowl. "Let's get on with things, then."

"How so?"

The woman shrugged. "If you want to kill me, go ahead. I deserve it. But make it quick. I won't beg for my life or say I deserve a second chance. I know I don't. I'll send you a postcard from hell, and I won't hold it against you. Of all the people in this world, you most of all deserve to kill someone like me. Maybe I didn't personally come after you, but I helped the order out in ways that led to it."

The bounty hunter whipped her gun out and aimed it at Drysi's head. "Alison told me you were the one who gave Conrad up," she explained, her voice calm even though her heart thumped.

"I did. He's a right bastard. Part of me helping out was because I was inspired by Alison, but I won't lie. A big part of it is also that Conrad's such an asshole that I want to see him annihilated, and Alison is the best bet for that. I hope he joins me in hell soon. I'd love to kill him myself." She closed her eyes. "Do it. I'm ready."

Neither woman breathed as she stood there, her gun aimed directly at Drysi's head. A single shot at this range would do it.

I have all the reasons in the world to do it. She said so herself. I'm not naïve, not like Alison. She might destroy dark wizards, but she's still that little teenager who sees the beauty in souls and ignores the darkness.

She sighed and lowered her gun. "I'm not going to kill you."

The witch opened her eyes. "You aren't?" She sounded surprised.

Izzie's chuckle sounded bitter. "I'm not hard enough despite that big speech. I can't execute someone in cold blood even if they deserve it, especially when they helped me out. If you want me to kill you, you'll have to try to kill me."

Drysi nodded and grabbed her jacket. She slipped it on and zipped it. "Everything I said before was true, even before the spell. I want to help destroy the Seventh Order, even if that is nothing more than helping you fight through a few guards when the time comes."

"If we do that, you might not survive."

"I was ready to die at your hands, and I'm ready to die if it means I can take some of them with me. I never expected to survive what happened on Nereid Island. Maybe God's given this right sinner a second chance."

"Maybe." She holstered her gun with a frown. "Conrad, Tabitha, Jeanne, and Zachariah."

The Welshwoman's eyebrows raised. "Are those the names of all the leaders? I served them for years, and I only ever knew about Conrad. There were always rumors about others, but it was hard to know the truth."

The bounty hunter nodded. "I got the last name earlier tonight. I think it's time we passed them along to someone who can do something with them." She pointed to the motorcycle, a Triumph Street Fighter. "We'll take the train to Seattle, and we'll hook up with Alison. Leave the bike in the parking lot with the keys. We won't need it where we're going."

Drysi sighed. "This isn't the same bike I had. I just bought it."

Izzie rolled her eyes.

"I can't wait until we see Alison again," her companion muttered.

CHAPTER SIXTEEN

Ava knocked lightly on the open office door. "I'm sorry to bother you, Miss Brownstone, but something important has come up. I know you're busy."

"This isn't exactly important stuff." Alison looked up with a smile. She had been perusing housing listings, which was fun but not all that critical. "What's up? I thought we were still waiting to hear from the client for the new job. I don't mind if they don't want to hire us. After that Drow crap, I could use a few weeks off. A few months off, actually, but if we wait too long, some new princess will show up to mess with us." She laughed nervously.

Her assistant gave her a thin smile. "Of course. I apologize, but I suspect you won't have time for a vacation for a few weeks." She glanced hastily over her shoulder. "I should perhaps have called ahead given the importance of your visitors, but it's an unusual circumstance, and I wanted to bring them right away and not have them linger in the lobby because of the additional risk of exposure."

"Guests? Risk of exposure?" She frowned. "I wasn't

expecting anyone." She winced and wondered if her dad had arrived to harass her and Mason about moving in together. Ava might simply be politely worrying about fangirls and fanboys swarming for a James Brownstone autograph.

If I keep things up, I might have the same problem, but something about Dad really seems to excite people. Maybe it's all the barbecue.

Ava opened the door wider and gestured for someone to enter. Not James Brownstone, though. Izzie and Drysi stood in the hallway, and both looked tired and a little dirty. Alison was reasonably sure there were a few small chunks of drywall in her friend's hair.

She jolted out of her chair. "What? This is…you aren't the two people I expected to see today. Drysi you're okay? You came here in broad daylight." She shook her head. "I have a thousand questions. You two are together?" She took another good look at them and held up her hand. "I know both of you have your own reasons to keep a low profile. Are you being pursued? I want to evacuate non-combat staff if necessary."

The bounty hunter shook her head. "I know I'm always on the run, but no one is hot on our tail at this exact moment." She nodded toward Drysi. "With her help, I already eliminated the latest batch. And you already fought off the Seventh Order here, so it's probably one of the safest semi-public places for me in Seattle. Anyway, I think I have what we need to finish this, and I think we should talk about it and what comes next."

Alison took a deep breath and exhaled slowly before she turned to the Welsh witch. "If you're here with Izzie, that means she's already done at least a decent job of checking you out. I should have known you weren't dead when they couldn't find your body." She smiled. "Are you here to help with the order?"

"You're bloody right I am."

She nodded at Ava. "Get the others. It's time for a little meeting."

"Right away, Miss Brownstone."

Hana waved to Izzie and Drysi as she stepped into the conference room, a cheerful smile on her face as if this was a get-together for a girls' night and not to discuss a fanatical dark wizard secret society.

This is serious, but at the same time, I'm happy to see Izzie again so soon. I'm even happy to know Drysi survived.

Mason's frown and glare made it clear what he thought of the Welshwoman, whereas he offered a polite nod to the bounty hunter. Tahir barely paid the newcomers any attention as he entered last. He tapped at his phone before he slid into his chair without looking up.

Ava closed the door behind the infomancer, seated herself near her boss, and positioned a tablet to take notes. She blended into the background in that way only she could manage.

Alison took a deep breath. "Let me make it clear upfront. We're about to talk about dark wizard crap. This isn't a client mission, and anyone who doesn't want to be involved doesn't have to be. I ask you as my friends, but I also understand the danger the Seventh Order represents, and I wouldn't blame any of you if you didn't want to deal with that kind of heat."

The fox rolled her eyes. "As if. Do you seriously think I'll run away with my tails tucked between my legs? Besides, this isn't only about you. Those dark wizard assholes attacked this building. They made it personal, and I look forward to being able to return the favor."

Mason nodded. "I'm with you, A. You know that."

Tahir shrugged. "I merely want a challenge. I don't care about the target, but I recommend we keep Sonya out of it. She's coming along well, but counter-tracking and counter-scrying is still a weakness of hers, and I'm dubious that the Seventh Order will show restraint because she's a child."

"Agreed," Alison responded and smiled. She wasn't surprised that her friends agreed to help, but it was still nice to hear them confirm their commitment. They already had a strong team gathered in the room. A few additions, including her dad, would make them unstoppable. She turned to Izzie. "Lay it out for us. Well, mostly for Tahir."

The infomancer looked at the bounty hunter with a faintly curious glint in his eyes. "Please provide the information you think is most relevant. And please, also consider that I don't care about the context."

"Conrad Barnes." She raised a single finger. "Tabitha Nelson. "Jeanne Martin, and Zachariah. Those are the top leaders of the Seventh Order." Another finger rose with each name.

Alison blew out a breath. "It's kind of strange."

"Strange?" Her friend frowned. "How?"

"They aren't simply faceless, scheming wizards, but

four actual people. Even knowing about Conrad wasn't the same. It's like we can finally see the face of our true enemy."

"And the plan?" Mason asked. "The PDA could contact sister agencies in the UK or wherever their base is. Their involvement in the Fremont Troll incident is terrorism."

Their leader shook her head. "They've done well to hide their trail. We can't walk up to the government and throw a few suspicions at them based on the testimony of a former member and a sketchy bounty hunter."

Izzie smirked. "I'm sketchy now?"

"Probably to the government, yeah." Alison sighed. "And I don't trust that there aren't Seventh Order sympathizers who might tip them off." She shook her head. "We need to be the ones who execute the decapitation strike."

The two newcomers exchanged curious looks.

What's that about?

Drysi focused on Alison. "And you're ready for that? You can't hesitate with these bastards, Alison. Mercy for them means more people dying. Are you ready to kill them?"

"I've been ready to kill them for a long time," she replied with a shrug.

What? Did those two have some sort of Alison's too soft chat?

Hana snickered quietly. "These dark wizards will be so surprised they'll wet themselves."

Mason leaned forward, concern on his face. "But are we sure it's enough? Assuming Tahir can find us the locations of those four and we take them out, won't they simply elect new guys or something?"

Drysi shook her head. She tapped her finger on the table.

"Everything I've found out suggests that if they're taken out, the order will crumble. It's one of the reasons they're all so bloody paranoid. They believe they have the weight of a sacred mission on their shoulders and all that rubbish. If we kill those four, the Seventh Order is finished, right tidy-like." She shook her head. "You need to understand the politics of the dark wizards. Every family thinks they should rule and that the group as a whole should rule, but that's supposed to be because they're better, smarter, and wiser. Many of them are ruthless by the average person's standards, but they aren't the kind of stone-cold killers you see in the Seventh Order. Most of them find the order a group of disagreeable hooligans."

Hana laughed. "Disagreeable hooligans?"

The witch snorted and shrugged.

Tahir typed in the names and curiosity washed the last hints of boredom from his face. "Fortunately, I've spent so much time already tracking Conrad Barnes, I believe it'll be fairly straightforward to connect him to others. I've grown weary of their analog arrogance, and I look forward to providing everything you need to attack them. If they are alienated from other dark wizards, that will only make this easier."

Izzie shrugged. "What good does knowing all that do? So not all dark wizards are complete assholes. They haven't stopped the Seventh Order, now, have they? I won't give them a cookie for only being arrogant and somewhat dangerous assholes rather than murderous maniacs."

"No, they haven't stopped Conrad and his mates, but they also won't go out of their way to help them either, nor will they avenge them. Several non-order dark families have suggested that the order should be blamed for focusing the attention of the Brownstone and Berens families so much on the dark families." Drysi gestured toward Alison. "Not only that, many of them have turned against the order because they think releasing a Mountain Strider was too much. Keep in mind, most of them also thought the Galbrathians were right assholes, too."

Hana muttered, "That's low-bar, but I'll take it."

"The bloody point is that the Seventh Order is all up its own ass with secrecy because they not only have to hide from the governments but also other dark families who might want to mess with them." Drysi pointed at her chest. "I was a member, and even I didn't know the identity of the other three leaders. If you take those bastards out, no one will know what's happening, and the others will take the opportunity to contain them if only to save their own asses."

Alison could almost see the hostility radiating off Mason as he glared at the witch.

"And we should believe you because of why exactly?" he asked. "Your initial involvement with Alison is proof that they'll try some clever tactics if they think it'll give them the advantage over their enemies."

"You have every right to not trust me, and I'm half-surprised you haven't killed me." She shrugged. "Anyway, I'll submit to truth magic. Whatever spells you need. You can search me as well. I won't offer any excuses. The only thing I want is to be there when you destroy Conrad, in particular. I owe the bastard and I owe his victims. I owe my victims."

Mason's frown turned into a cold smile. "You can lead from the front, then, Drysi."

Alison blinked a few times, unused to seeing him quite so vicious.

I get that he's worried about me, but he's going Dad-level protective here. I need to dial things down.

"I'll take whatever resources we can get," she interjected.

The life wizard drew in a deep breath through his nose and replied with a curt nod.

Tahir stood and headed toward the door.

"Where are you going?" she asked.

He stopped and looked over his shoulder. "I presume you want me to track everyone immediately, correct?"

"Yeah. Do it." She nodded and turned to Ava. "Why don't you go with him and see if there's anything you can do on your end to help him? The quicker we find all these assholes, the quicker this thing is over."

Even if Ava wasn't an infomancer, the administrative assistant did have a knack for turning up information— probably learned from her likely past as an intelligence operative.

Maybe that's what she wants us to think, and she was never a spy at all. It'd be funny if it turned out she simply decided to be the world's most kick-butt assistant.

The woman stood and nodded politely. "Of course, Miss Brownstone."

The two hurried out and Alison surveyed her remaining allies. "He's right. If he comes back five minutes later and tells me they're all together, I want to move ASAP."

"Shouldn't we call a few more people?" Hana asked. "I'm not suggesting you aren't tough, but two Brownstones are better than one. It's too bad your mom can't come to play." She sighed.

"What's wrong with Shay?" Izzie frowned.

"Nothing," Alison explained. "She's pregnant."

"Oh. Uh, congratulations." The bounty hunter shook her head, a shocked expression on her face. She dug in her pocket and retrieved a small, polished quartz crystal and tossed it to her friend. "I'll head out soon, so I wanted you to have this."

"What's this?" She eyed the crystal, but there weren't any glyphs or symbols on it.

"Something I found recently. It has a single use only, though. Squeeze it and channel some magic into it, and it'll call for me. I suppose you could think of it as a magical beeper. Now that I brought your little witch here, I'll lay low. I'm something of an ambush magnet lately." Izzie shrugged. "I'll stay local in case Tahir finds something soon." She looked from Drysi to Alison, an uneasy expression on her face. "But I'm with you. I want this over, and soon."

Mason nodded toward the witch. "A truth spell isn't good enough. We have to be careful until we're ready to go."

The half-Drow frowned. "You don't think so?"

Hana sighed. "I hate to sound like a bitch, but I agree. She might be on Team Brownstone right now, but we have no guarantees that it's permanent."

Drysi frowned. "I don't blame you, but I also don't know what else I can do to prove I'm on your side."

"I suppose it's a good way to test out the containment cell." She smiled apologetically. "It's something I wanted added after the dark wizard attacked this place before, but I haven't really used it and they only recently finished construction. I refuse to use Chesterton-tech anti-magic emitters, but the walls are impregnated with anti-magic crystal material, and the outer area is warded with Myna's help. I might not be able to keep a Mountain Strider in there, but it should easily hold one witch without her wand."

"Fair enough, but does this mean I won't be there in the end?" Drysi's voice held a note of desperation.

Alison shook her head. "No. When we locate them, you'll have your chance, too. For now, we let Tahir do his thing. Once he has information, we gather the rest of our allies and we finish the Seventh Order."

CHAPTER SEVENTEEN

Alison groaned as her eyes flickered open. A deep darkness smothered her, the product of the cloudy Seattle night and her blackout curtains.

Wait. Why am I awake? It's the middle of the damned night.

A soft trill sounded. She blinked her weary eyes and finally realized it was the sound of her phone ringing.

Someday, I should set it up so it routes all my night calls to Ava so she can handle them. She probably wouldn't even care.

Immediately, she frowned. There was the small problem of Ava contacting her after that.

With another extended groan, she fumbled on the nightstand to find the offending device. She peered at it and the cloudiness in her head vanished when she saw the call was from Tahir.

Could he have found something that fast?

Mason muttered something as he sat up and squinted in the darkness at the bright phone screen that illuminated their bed. "What's going on?"

"Tahir," she explained and moved the phone to her ear. "What's up, Tahir?" she asked, her voice still croaky with sleep. "This isn't another one of those things where you forgot that not everyone has the same attitude toward sleep that you do, is it?"

He snorted. "Of course not, and that hasn't happened for, what, two weeks? This is one of those things where I've collected critical time-sensitive intelligence you can use against your enemies to destroy them—enemies that have hounded you and your friend Izzie for years."

Excitement blasted the remaining fatigue from Alison's mind. She swallowed and her heart pounded.

It's not a dream. We're there. We're damned there!

Alison activated speaker mode and lowered the phone. "I've put you on speaker with Mason. Give me what you have."

"You'll forgive me," Tahir replied, "as I did not wake Hana. I don't think she needs to be awake for this part, though. She's far less interested in the considerations of tactical planning. I'm sure we can all agree on that."

She yawned. "It's fine. What did you find?"

"Although I want to go through why my methods were brilliant in terms of their techniques and execution, for purposes of brevity, I'll simply explain that having four targets instead of one made it far easier to track them despite their attempts at obfuscation and misdirection. That is, they all hid things in the same kind of way, which made it, ironically, more obvious that they were hiding things."

"Okay. A little typical dark wizard arrogance to help us along. I can work with that." She licked her lips to ease the dryness. "Are you telling me you know where all four of them are?"

"Yes," the infomancer replied. "I know where they are and where they'll be in the next few days."

"So we know where they are. This can work. We'll have enough heavy hitters to put together four teams. All we have to do is strike simultaneously. That way, they can't reinforce one another, and they won't know what's going on." She glanced at her boyfriend who nodded his approval.

Tahir chuckled. "That's a fascinating plan, but I can assure you it's also completely and utterly unnecessary—in addition to being more complicated and prone to failure."

Mason rubbed his eyes and shuffled into a more comfortable position. "Would you care to explain why, or do you prefer to simply be smug about it?"

The other man snorted. "In this case, my smugness is justified because my work has led to a breakthrough. I will note that Ava contributed a few suggestions concerning some data sources I should check, which proved surprisingly helpful, but it was still fundamentally my skills and effort that brought us this unique victory."

Alison scrubbed a hand over her face. Tahir could monologue worse than a supervillain at times. "Why isn't the damned plan necessary? Spell it out for me, please. I'm still half-asleep."

"Such impatience," Tahir scoffed. "It isn't necessary, Alison, because all four of the leaders of the Seventh Order will gather together for a meeting in a few days. They will all be in the same location for at least one day."

She released a sharp yelp of victory. "You're fucking kidding me."

"No. I'm simply that skilled at what I do. I imagine throwing a large, combined force at them will be far easier than four separate coordinated groups."

Honestly, she could almost taste the condescension over the phone, but she would let him hold onto that for the moment. He was about to deliver exactly what they needed to free Izzie and end the dark wizard threat.

"Where?" she asked, her voice filled with excitement. Not even a hint of tiredness or sleep remained. "I know we won't be so lucky as to have them gather on some abandoned island, but it would be nice."

"No, not an abandoned island," Tahir replied.

Alison sighed. "Please tell me it's not in the middle of London. I'd like to do this without too many government people involved. Not only that, some of my contacts can paper over trouble if it's minor, but if Big Ben gets blown up or something, that'll be a lot harder to explain away."

"Big Ben will not be a concern. We're discussing Canada, not England."

That definitely was not what she'd expected, and she frowned. "Huh? Canada?"

"They aren't meeting in England," the informancer explained with exaggerated patience. "The more one thinks about it, the more it makes sense. They aren't all English, so there's no particular reason for them to meet in England other than the fact that Conrad has so much influence there. Izzie merely happened to attract some stronger trails there for that reason, but the same thing might have happened in Paris."

"And you're sure they'll be in Canada?" Mason interjected.

"Yes," Tahir responded, a hint of weary irritation in his voice. "Or, to be more specific, they will meet in a mansion in the outskirts of Vancouver. I've done discreet collection and hacking to acquire current and historical satellite imagery, and it's very obvious to me that they have some kind of illusion over the place. I'm dubious of flying a drone or using a scrying spell, as there's too much risk of direct detection."

Energized by a renewed sense of purpose, Alison slid out of bed. There was no way she would sleep after this conversation. "Good instincts. If we have them all there together, we need to make sure we don't do anything that spooks them. We might not have another chance like this for months." She paced beside the bed, the dim light of the phone the only illumination. "Why do you think they have an illusion over the place?"

"It's taken some coordination of satellite images, but there's insufficient activity there. It looks like a place that is well-maintained, but I've not seen, for example, any gardeners in action or evidence of magic. Somehow, it's always conveniently mowed regardless of when the image is taken. No one comes in or out, which is suspicious, and some IR imagery I've retrieved is remarkably and consistently even."

"Are you sure?" Mason asked. "Wouldn't someone have noticed?"

The infomancer scoffed. "Why would they? Many satellites constantly monitor almost the entire Earth, and unless someone has a reason to look at a particular area, even with magic and computers, there's a lot of imagery to go through. If you didn't already know a particular mansion was odd, why bother to spend time examining their gardening schedule?"

Alison flipped the light on. "This is another advantage then. It means the Seventh Order has every reason to believe they'll be safe and will have their guard down. They think they have everyone fooled, including the US and Canadian governments. If anyone has caught on, they probably had their people planted inside the government agencies handle it." She rubbed her hand together, her heart racing. "And you said this place is on the outskirts of town and is a mansion? That makes it sound like there are no other large buildings around."

"That would be accurate, yes. There are outbuildings and the like associated with the mansion, but no other occupied structure for several miles. I suspect they use portals to travel directly to and from the location."

Mason slid out of bed and grabbed his T-Shirt off the nightstand. "They probably aren't the hiding in plain sight kind of guys. That works for us." He shrugged. "We could simply blow them away from a distance."

She shook her head firmly. "They might have hostages or prisoners in there for all we know. We'll have to still go in there and clear it manually. You said the meeting's in a few days?"

"Yes, three days, unless the message I uncovered is intended to be misleading."

"Nope. They haven't played with that kind of deception." She grinned. "Three days, huh? It gives me plenty of time to bring in the rest of our team."

The following morning, Alison waved a keycard over the containment cell lock and it clicked open.

Drysi sat on the small bed she'd been lying on. "I've only been in here a day and you're letting me out? Is this time off for good behavior?"

"If I trust you to fight at my side, it seems pointless to lock you up." She shrugged.

"Your friends don't trust me much and I can't say that they're wrong." The witch stood, threaded her hands together, and stretched her arms above her head. "After everything I've done and how much I've lied, I would never trust me."

She sighed and shook her head. "And that's why my side —the good guys or the light families or whatever you want to call us—will always win against the dark families in the long run."

A hint of amusement passed over her companion's face. "What do you mean by that?"

"Paranoia doesn't lead to good team building. It's as simple as that. The people who work for me do so because they like me and I value them as people, not as tools or pawns."

"Don't you remember the old joke, Alison? It's not paranoia when they are out to get you." Drysi winked and lowered her arms.

"True, but there are a lot of good people out there who have made mistakes and deserve a chance to atone for them. Even Rhazdon, in the end, realized she had made mistakes." She sighed and stepped away from the open cell.

"I'd rather be wrong on occasion than live in a world where I think I can't save someone if they're willing to be saved."

The Welshwoman sauntered out of the cell. "You can't save Conrad and his mates, you know that, right? If you're harboring some delusion of talking them out of their plans, it's exactly that—a delusion. There's only one right and tidy way to solve this. You kill them."

Alison scoffed. "I'm not exactly a pacifist. I'll do what I need to. These people have screwed with me for a long time. All I'm saying is that I choose to trust you. Aside from the fact that you passed Izzie's tests, you had plenty of opportunities to screw with me or her." She gestured to the vest and leather jacket that lay on a nearby stark black table. "The order wants Izzie most of all. I'm almost incidental in all this. If you intended to betray someone, you would have taken the chance already."

"And if you're wrong?"

She grinned widely. "I was wrong about you before, and you still did the right thing."

Drysi slipped the vest on and zipped it slowly. "This time, it's as much about vengeance as it is about justice. I'm not you, Alison. I'm not a good person. I'm merely not a complete monster like Conrad."

"I've known many people who were terrible before they became good people." Alison headed toward the door. "When you start on the bottom, there's no place to go but up. Let Ava know if you need any special equipment. If you want to practice, you can access our tactical training room. We'll make our move soon."

"And what will you do?"

She grabbed the door handle and paused. "I'll contact a few people for help."

CHAPTER EIGHTEEN

L ily bent back and her flexibility allowed her to form an almost perfect ninety-degree angle. The move was great for limbo—and also helped to avoid flaming blades that erupted from walls.

The blazing trap hissed and spun less than an inch over her nose. It lodged in the dirt wall of the cavern with a mighty, reverberating thud.

For all she knew, it also had poison on it given that it was already overkill as both a blaze and a sharp blade. She'd encountered stranger things in her career as a tomb raider, but some of the absurdities never sat well with her, even if she was a half-Gray Elf who could see partially into the future.

She took a deep breath and released it slowly. Thankfully, she'd timed the future check perfectly.

To rush out of the cavern would get her killed. There was still too much interference to contact Celia—not that her support could do much to help her if she was decapitated or even severely wounded.

The tomb raider straightened, wiped the sweat off her face, and fumbled behind her in the pocket of her backpack. The object of her quest, a small enchanted figurine, remained safely inside.

"Maybe I need an apprentice," Lily mumbled. "Someone who specializes in sewing heads back on. I helped Shay more than a few times when shit got real, and those jerks from Hollingsworth have entire teams. But here I am, wandering around this cavern filled with ridiculously lethal traps, and I don't have anyone with me."

She sighed and continued down the path that would lead her out of the cavern and paused often to use her ability to see what might lie ahead. Despite the temptation to use it more, she had to pace herself to ensure she didn't get lost in the future. Her near-death experience had encouraged a more deliberate pace.

Sometimes, she didn't know if she preferred how her power used to work before she had refined it. She could control it now, which made it more useful in some ways, but the time horizon was far shorter. It was nice to sometimes know of an ambush or trap more than a few minutes in advance. Maybe if she could still do that, she wouldn't have ended up a prisoner in Japan.

Celia had suggested her boss take a few months off after everything that had happened in Kyoto. Harry felt the same, but she insisted that she needed another job, and soon, to both her support person and her fiancé. She didn't mind having to give up the mirror, but it was damned embarrassing that her friend had to come and rescue her. Not only that, but if anything had happened to Alison or any of her people, Lily wouldn't have been able to forgive herself.

It would be nice to have a partner. Celia's great, but there are so many times when I'm stuck in a cave with nothing but my thoughts. Or maybe Harry's right and I should give it up. It's not like we need the money anymore.

She rubbed her arms. While she liked to believe she wasn't addicted to danger, she also tried to be honest with herself. Those two commitments often conflicted.

The cave path turned and narrowed. The acrid scent of burned moss along with scorch marks on the walls were the evidence of an earlier trap she'd avoided on her way inside. No blades or poison were involved with that one, though.

The tomb raider heaved a deep breath, concentrated, and blinked as the scene ahead wavered, only to be replaced by what she actually saw. The immediate future was nothing more than the same empty cave. Grateful for the assurance, she restored her usual focus and continued.

The minutes blurred together as she followed the serpentine cave path. Her own shallow footprints provided an easy trail out.

A humanoid shadow appeared unexpectedly around a nearby corner. She whipped her gun out, crouched, and narrowed her eyes. A future check with someone in the vicinity was tempting but not worth the risk. Getting lost now might kill her.

Damn it. Another tomb raider? Celia didn't find anything to suggest that there were any intelligent inhabitants in the cave.

Alison stepped into view. A light orb floated above her, and she shimmered slightly. "Oh, there you are, Lily. I thought I would have to walk deep into this place." She made a face. "I guess this is better than wandering through some cockroach-infested underground maze but not by much."

Lily holstered her weapon. "Is this a new thing? You wander into random caves in Indonesia now?"

"Maybe it should be. That sounds like a fun way to travel the world." Her friend chuckled. "By the way, remember that time I saved your life?" she joked. "I'm not saying I'll use it to force you to do anything you don't want to do, but I thought I'd bring it up."

"It was oh, so long ago—a whole couple of weeks and all." She rolled her eyes. "Why? Or do you simply feel like messing with me?"

"Nope." The half-Drow looked thoughtful for a moment. "If anything, it was interesting to face a group of magicals who were different than what I was used to. We have many magicals in Seattle, but they tend to be the most common types from Oriceran and Earth. Japan, though— that was almost a working vacation."

She laughed. "I'll try to only be captured in interesting places, or maybe next time, I'll do...Antarctica." Her laughter died down. "Wait. Celia didn't call you in, did she? I told her I might need a few extra hours." She rolled her eyes. "She's become super-worried since Japan. You'd think she was the one in the damned cave."

Alison shook her head. "I tried to get hold of you and contacted her when I couldn't. She told me where you were, so I had a friend open a portal for me because I had to talk to you."

"You had to talk to me right away?"

"I'm on a tight timeline over the next few days. I'll drive back with you to the airport and we can supersonic back to Seattle. I'll pay."

"What about your friend with the portal?"

Her friend's smile vanished. "It's best if she's judicious in her use of magic for several reasons."

The tomb raider shrugged. "Fair enough. If you've come looking for me, I can only assume you need me for something. What? Are you too much of a bounty-hunting city girl to raid a sewer?"

"It's time," she announced. "Time to take out the dark wizards. I hoped you would help."

Lily whistled. "Maybe I should run back into the cave."

"Hey, do you still have that Assyrian clay top you told me about?" Alison asked.

She grinned. "Yes, yes, I do."

Myna scoffed and folded her arms obdurately. She rose from the couch, cold fury in her eyes. "I absolutely refuse to accept what you just said."

Alison sighed from where she sat somewhat stiffly in her recliner. She'd expected this reaction, but that didn't make it any easier to hear it. "All I said was that this won't be a few spells. I know what it's like to have AMDS and go into battle with it, and you'll do your part anyway. We don't need you to fight people. It's not a big deal."

"And you thought I would accept things if you explained it that way?" the woman harrumphed. "You're far too intelligent to believe such idiocy. It is as I said."

She held a hand up in an effort to placate her mentor. "I don't get why you're so obsessed with actually joining the battle. I take missions all the time—dangerous missions—and you don't seem to care. You weren't offended when I jetted off to Japan and didn't ask you to come along."

"Your security mercenary activity isn't a true risk. That's why people hire you. This Seventh Order is a different matter, and Japan was a rescue mission, not an extermination. These wizards represent a serious threat to you, my princess. To ask me to stand aside while you and your comrades risk yourselves in a deadly battle against men who have attacked you repeatedly is an insult. I would even be willing to attack them myself."

Alison shook her head. "You already have a crippling disease because of me. You've advised and taught me and made me a better Drow. But this could end up with you dead because you're overwhelmed by pain in the middle of the battle. I don't want to set you up to die."

Myna stared at her for a long moment and almost looked disappointed. "I've not taught you enough, it seems, about what it truly means to be a Drow. If I'm to die, I'd rather fall in battle while killing the enemies of my princess than simply go to sleep and never awaken. Death comes for me soon, regardless of how I hide from her. If she wants to arrive sooner, so be it. I will not accept exclusion from this battle. If you have any respect for me at all, you'll understand that."

"And what if I ordered you not to participate as the Princess of the Shadow Forged?" Alison locked eyes with the ancient Drow in a challenge.

Her companion's jaw tightened. "It would be a grave

insult. Do you wish to deny a dying old woman one of her last wishes? Does your desire to shield me from an inevitable death outweigh my dignity?"

"Dying old woman?" She groaned and slumped down in her chair. "Did you seriously pull that card?"

"It's the truth, isn't it? I am dying, and I am old, and I wish to fight by your side in a true battle. If I perish in the fight or even a short moment after, I die knowing that I fought beside a great woman—and that you see me as a Drow and not some dying ancient who needs to be protected."

Alison released a long, defeated sigh. "Everyone said this is how you would react."

"Then they understand better than you do."

"I don't even know why I bothered to think I could talk you out of it."

Shay leaned forward to give James a long, deep kiss. She pulled away with a suspicious look on her face.

"Remember." She shook her finger. "Stay under modified Forerunner. Normally, I wouldn't care so much, but I don't want any annoying bullshit while I'm pregnant, and you starting a war with the US government counts as annoying bullshit. Wait at least…uh, I don't know…six to eight weeks afterward. The baby should sleep more than a few hours by that point."

"I don't need that Forerunner shit," James grunted in protest. "This isn't a bunch of Vax or even weird-ass demons. These are merely dark wizard assholes. I probably won't even do that much. If I push too hard, I might make Alison and Izzie all pissed thinking I haven't left anyone for them." He shrugged. "It can't even be that big a deal if the Fixer and Berens aren't coming."

"Alison made it clear that it's not that they don't give a shit, but more that they're up to their necks in some other shit." Shay sighed. "Damn, I wish I could go, but I don't want to take any chances. This is annoying and exactly like the Battle of LA. I have to sit out the best part."

Her husband shrugged but did try to look vaguely sympathetic. "I'm sure it won't be that much fun, but at least it gives Whispy something to do. Sometimes I feel bad, but he never bitches more than I can handle. I asked him if he even perceives time when we're not bonded, and he gave some weird-ass symbiont answer I don't understand that sounds like he's saying yes and no at the same time."

"Are you sure about not including anyone from the agency? Trey's gonna be pissed when he finds out he wasn't invited to the party. Or what about May? She's all about confronting dark wizard types. The other guys too." She regarded him with a slight frown that almost looked hopeful.

James shook his head. "I can't ask them to do that."

"No, you can't order them to do it, but you can ask them."

"I don't need all my employees and friends to help my daughter." He squared his shoulders. "There haven't been many times I've been able to kick ass for Alison, and almost all those times were fucking defense against the Drow."

Shay gave him a suspicious look. "Oh, this is you proving some sort of point?"

"This is me being a good father."

"By brutally killing a group of wizards?" She raised an eyebrow.

He grunted and looked a little smug as he patted her stomach. "Exactly. I promise, we'll take a few his-and-hers ass-kickings next year, but for now, I'll kick enough ass for you, me, Trey, and everyone else at the agency." He opened the door.

"What if Extended Advanced isn't enough?" his wife asked quietly.

"Then I go full Forerunner. No big mystery."

"Even if it pisses the government off?"

"Fuck the government. There's nothing more important than my family." James stepped outside and headed toward his F-350. "Although my truck's close," he murmured.

"I heard that shit, James!" she yelled.

"I said it's close, not more important."

CHAPTER NINETEEN

Alison surveyed the conference room. While she'd seen it full any number of times when Jerry and the field support team joined the meetings, there had never been so many enhanced individuals in the room at one time.

Tahir, her dad, Hana, Mason, Lily, Izzie, Drysi, and Myna all sat around the table. Ava wasn't at the meeting today, which made James technically the only non-magical there—but he was most definitely not a normal human being.

Most of them have never seen what he can do up close.

James grunted as he looked around. "What was up with all the park far away and enter through a portal shit? Why couldn't I drive here? If I had to go through a fucking portal, I wouldn't have driven my truck all the way up here. And I hate portals."

"You hate anything that's not a Ford truck, Dad," his daughter responded. "And the reason is because we don't know how closely the Seventh Order might be watching this place. The building itself is heavily warded, but they might be suspicious if they see you, Izzie, Lily, and Myna all walk into the building around the same time. It was risky enough when Izzie and Drysi arrived the other day. For our attack to work, they can't be alerted at all."

"Why not use an illusion?" Hana asked. "Like they're doing on the mansion? Between all the people gathered here, you should be able to pull it off."

Alison shook her head. "It'd be too obvious with all the people who come and go on a daily basis. For now, the portals were the best options, and if all goes well, this shit will be over in a few hours anyway." She spared a glance at Myna.

I wish I didn't have to put her through that pain, but she's the only person we have who can make the damn things. Maybe I should hire someone specifically for that.

Lily shifted restlessly in her chair, her frown persistent. "And are we sure these guys are still at the mansion? It'd be sad if we all knocked on the door to find no one home. There's nothing sadder than a party that got canceled."

Tahir frowned. "I can't fully verify if they are there or not without risking detection. No vehicles have been observed entering or leaving the premises. All we know is that the information I uncovered suggests all four leaders should be there until tomorrow morning. I have little evidence to suggest that they might be there longer than that."

Alison nodded. "We'll assume they're there, and we'll strike hard and fast. We won't have to worry about where they might be after tomorrow morning. So, let's go over the plan."

"It's difficult to plan without knowing their defenses. We're effectively walking in there blind," Mason pointed out.

James grunted. "Planning's overrated. Don't be a pussy."

She glared at her dad and gave him her best "don't start this shit now" look. He shrugged. Shay had apparently worked to soften him toward accepting that Mason and Alison would move in together, but it didn't seem like it had worked much.

And everything went so well when they first met.

Drysi cleared her throat and spoke tentatively. "Seventh Order typically has a group of low-rent wizards and witches and at best, a few mercs. Conrad, in particular, doesn't like his people too talented. He's too paranoid to have people around whom he suspects might be better than him, but I don't know about the others."

"Anyone else they might use?" Alison asked. It sounded too simplistic and she couldn't help but wonder if they had missed anything

"I've seen them use Oriceran mercs, too—like Zain, on occasion—but if this place is one of their special buildings, they'll want to keep it pure. They really believe in the great history and traditions of the dark wizard families. If they can find shifter mercenaries who will work hire on, they like to use them as well."

"I've seldom run into extra help like that when I've fought them," she replied. "But we might have to worry about enhancing artifacts like they used when I fought them in DC." She glanced at her dad. "I doubt they'd have anything that could hurt you, though. It's not new magic from what I've seen."

James shrugged. "I'm only here to clear shit out so you can have a Brownstone chat with the motherfuckers who started this." He nodded to Izzie. "Sorry, Berens too, but first-come, first-served."

The bounty hunter smirked. "Don't worry, Mr. Brownstone. I don't care how they die, only that they do actually die and I get my damned life back."

"Good." He grunted with a look that suggested he was ready to make it happen. "That makes shit simpler and that's always better. If we need to, I'll make them concentrate on me. I don't give two shits if it pisses off the Canadian or American governments. They should do a better fucking job of keeping homicidal wizards in check so we don't have to come in and clean their shit up for them."

Drysi eyed him speculatively. "It's true, then. I've heard that you're basically immune to almost everything once you get going, and even if someone cuts your arm off, it'll grow back. That's a nice and tidy artifact you have. I'm surprised you listen to the government at all."

"I mind my own business—most of the time, anyway. This is special for my daughter." He leaned forward. "And I know all about you too, Jones. If you try any shit, I will kill you where you stand. I'm not as nice as Alison."

She responded with a feral grin. "Good. Besides, I won't lie. If I have to die, it'd be impressive to be killed by James Brownstone. Here lies Drysi Jones, brilliant witch, beautiful woman, and important enough to be killed by the Granite Ghost himself."

Alison cleared her throat to refocus the meeting. "Let's stay on task. Tahir, I want you and Sonya to concentrate on active monitoring of the Brownstone building. When we launch an assault against them, they might use the opportunity to return the favor. With the anti-magic equipment we have here, I'm confident that Jerry and his team can hold out long enough for AET to arrive, but having infomancer support will make an enormous difference—exactly like it did during the last attack."

Tahir sighed with the weary boredom of a child being told he couldn't see his favorite movie until after he'd done his homework. "I suppose you're right, but are you sure you won't need help there? I'm sure you could disrupt their spells with your initial attack so I could use drones or scrying windows."

"Help with the team I've gathered?" She chuckled. "Unless the Seventh Order are hiding a doomsday jar or something like that somewhere, the only question will be how long it takes to find Conrad and his buddies. The problem is that we don't have good intelligence about their forces, so we'll have to assume there is a shitload of wizards there, ready and able to defend their masters. That means a lightning strike with everything we have." She looked at Mason. "Aerial insertion?"

He frowned. "We can't fit everyone in the chopper, and no one else can fly."

Myna raised her chin and pride filled her eyes. "It's simple. I'll open a portal. I can create one right outside the edge of their illusion. The power of your allies is impressive, my princess, but they are small in number. It would be easy."

Hana scratched her chin and leaned forward. Her gaze darted from one team member to another. "That makes sense, but aren't we missing the obvious?"

"Which is what?" Alison asked.

"What if they're chicken?" The fox shrugged and everyone stared at her like she had lost her mind.

"Chicken?" their leader echoed.

She nodded. "If a team like ours knocked on our door, I don't know if I would stick around to fight them. That's all I'm saying."

James released a long, low growl. "I'll fucking level that place to the ground if they run."

Alison nodded toward Lily. The tomb raider retrieved a small, cracked clay top from her pocket and placed it on the table.

"Lily has that taken care of, but only if we don't turn this into some protracted slog." She gestured to object.

Mason leaned forward to peer closer at it. "Is that an artifact?"

"It disrupts portals and their formation," the Gray Elf explained. "But it only has enough power to last one hour, and this is a one-use item based on what I know of it. So we can keep the bastards there, but we'll have less than an hour to find and stop them before they can escape. Unless, of course, they try the old-fashioned way, but I'm sure we can blow up a few cars or trucks."

"We need to stop them there." Alison sighed. "Otherwise, we'll have to find the four leaders again and recruit enough wizards and witches so we could disrupt portals in a wide area. That would probably mean PDA involvement, which is too much of a risk."

James shook his head. "Nah. If we can go in there through Myna's portal and we can block their escape, we can finish this shit today. An hour? Fuck that. Let's finish it in fifteen minutes."

Drysi grinned. "I like his attitude."

Alison clapped sharply. "Okay, then. Let's arm and armor up. In two hours, we'll bring Seventh Order to their knees and chop their heads off."

James leaned against a wall while he waited for the team to prepare. He hadn't bothered to bring anything but Whispy. The symbiont was all the equipment he needed for an extermination mission. After a moment, the weight of someone's stare drew his attention to his right to where the ancient, wrinkled Drow woman stood a few yards away.

"What?" he rumbled. "Do you see something interesting?"

Myna nodded. "It's interesting to spend more time around you."

"Why the fuck do you care about me?"

"You are the man who defeated Laena." She gave him a tight smile.

"So?" James grunted, a little annoyed by the uninvited attention. "That bitch exiled you. I would have thought you were glad I kicked her ass."

"Oh, I'm very glad." Her smile softened with genuine warmth. "If you hadn't defeated her, she would have taken my princess to Oriceran and molded her into something as twisted as she was." Her smile faltered. "Alison's power is too great for her to risk corruption. With the girl to do her bidding, Laena would have led the Drow even farther down a path that mocked their true Drow nature."

He nodded slowly, still reticent. "You know I don't give a shit about the Drow. If they had left me alone, I would never have gone after Laena."

"I understand that, but your motivations are less relevant than what you accomplished." Myna blew out a short breath. "She would make a fine queen. I know she is young, but she is special."

"You don't have to tell me that, but being special and wanting to be queen are two separate things. She doesn't want to be queen."

"Sometimes, duty calls to us." She placed a hand over her heart. "Does not your pride as a father demand she take her throne?"

James chuckled at what he suspected might well be a ploy to win his support. "I'm proud of Alison no matter what she does, and I want her to be happy. I don't think she would be happy as Queen of the Drow."

Disappointment spread across the wrinkled features. "You're a curious being, James Brownstone. I suppose I shouldn't be surprised by your attitude."

"Why is that?"

"I've studied you on your Internet and I've spoken with your daughter about you." Myna shook her head. "You're a man who defeated Laena when you were less powerful. You're even more powerful now. You could become a king."

"That shit sounds boring and complicated." He shrugged as what little interest he'd had in the conversation faded. "I've never wanted to be in charge of anything.

My agency only runs effectively because it's overseen by a group of people smarter than me, and I have managers who deal with all the annoying shit for my restaurant."

"Such power, and you honestly don't wish to wield it to conquer?" Her tone approached reverential. "No wonder my princess knows such dedication and restraint."

James shook his head. "You have it all wrong."

"Oh?" A knowing smile appeared on her face. "You do seek control?"

"No, not that. I mean about Alison. She's always been a good person, and she made *me* better, not the other way around. That's why I have to help protect her." He slid a hand in under his jacket and retrieved his amulet. It was circular, gold and silver, and connected to a silver chain around his neck. Three crystals lay within—blue, red, and green. "You're gonna take us to that mansion, and we're gonna kill every motherfucker there. We're gonna make sure no dark wizard thinks about fucking with my daughter for the next five hundred years."

Myna nodded. "I am honored to join the battle in defense of my princess, Mr. Brownstone."

"Let's kick ass." He extended his hand. "Thanks for everything you do for her."

"May our enemies die at our hands and our deaths be glorious," she responded, and her handshake was surprisingly firm and strong.

CHAPTER TWENTY

The strike team stood in a wide hallway of the Brownstone Building. They were armed and ready to initiate the assault against the Seventh Order.

There would be no capture, no mercy, and no last chances. This was a concerted attack on the headquarters of a ruthless enemy that had repeatedly threatened them. Alison wouldn't kill anyone who surrendered, but she had no intention to pull any punches.

She had given a last-minute assignment to Tahir that he found more satisfying than waiting around and babysitting the building in case of invasion. It had occurred to her that they didn't want the Vancouver Anti-Magical Tactical Unit to show up in the middle of the party. They might not have time to ascertain the facts and could fire on the Brownstone team. The illusion, she hoped, would keep any local police away, but if it fell, it would be up to Tahir to stall them as long as possible. That, hopefully, would be long enough for her and her team on the ground to eliminate the leaders of the Seventh Order.

Lily grinned as she patted the magazines filled with anti-magic bullets tucked into the pouches on her tactical vest. "It's always more fun to spend other people's money. I usually try to keep it to one mag on my jobs. They eat into the profit margin."

Drysi laughed. "You're right." She slapped an anti-magic magazine into her gun and holstered it. Two dozen glowing throwing knives were sheathed in her vest. "It's also fun to have a fight where I don't have to give two shits about who I'm fighting. I do so enjoy it when the people I'm about to kill are worse than me."

"True enough." James grunted what might have been a laugh.

Hana rubbed her thumb over the hilt of her sword and looked thoughtful. "Sometimes, I wonder if I should use a two-sword style. It'd look much cooler."

"With your fox speed and the *tachi*, you're doing fine," Mason assured her.

She gasped. "Oh! Do you know what I just realized?"

They all froze and looked at her with concern.

"There are seven of us! Isn't that awesome? We should have a nickname like the Magnificent Seven." She bobbed her head, a huge smile on her face.

The life wizard laughed. "That one's taken."

"The Seven Brownstones?"

Lily laughed. "I'm not a Brownstone and I don't work for one."

"I'll come up with something. Cool nicknames are important." The fox grinned and winked before her eyes turned vulpine and her nine glowing tails appeared. "Let's kick some major ass."

All the magicals activated their shields or relevant artifacts except James.

Myna drew a deep breath. "I'm ready, my princess."

"Dad, you probably should gear up before we head through the portal," Alison suggested. "For all we know, the first thing they'll do is throw a bomb at us."

"Fine." He removed his jacket and tossed it on the floor. His jeans and T-shirt came next.

"Bloody hell," Drysi shouted. "A Brownstone strip show. Nice muscles there, Mr. Brownstone."

Alison made a face. "That's my dad."

"He's not my bloody dad."

Soon, the only garments remaining were a pair of boxer shorts and his amulet around his neck. A small metal spacer was taped to the back and separated it from his chest.

He shrugged. "My amulet shreds everything when I go even remotely full-out." He yanked the spacer off and hissed as the artifact sank halfway into his flesh. Tendrils burrowed beneath his skin and spread across and deeper into his chest.

Everyone but Alison and Myna grimaced. Newfound respect filled Mason's eyes.

"Damn," Lily muttered. "I've never actually seen him activate it before. That looks painful. Very painful."

James knelt and took three small gold chains from his discarded jeans. He pressed them against the amulet. "I need a little fuel other than anger."

The chains were likely minor magical artifacts supplied to him by either Shay or one of his witch employees.

Silver-green tendrils erupted from the amulet and

covered his body in a matter of seconds to coat him in armor of the same color with a metallic sheen. An eyeless helmet wrapped around his head. Two long, thin silver-green blades that resembled a mixture of bone and metal extended from his arms, and claws grew from his fingertips.

Hana gasped. "Wow. That is both simultaneously the most awesome thing I've ever seen in person and the freakiest. And I saw an umbrella ghost not all that long ago."

Her own skin glowed red from the use of the crystalline ring.

James craned his neck and twisted it to ease the transformation. "This is extended advanced mode. Think of it like eighty percent power. That should be enough for these fuckers."

"How do you see in that helmet?" Drysi asked and studied it curiously. "Or does it make you telepathic or something?"

He shook his head. "The helmet's almost like a camera. I have a wider range of vision—not quite three-sixty, but a lot more than normal."

"That's eighty percent power?" Mason asked, a hint of awe in his voice. "What is a hundred like?"

"The government doesn't like me to use a hundred percent. Don't worry. I don't need that shit for a few dark wizards, and I have a few new tricks even at this power level." He rasped his blades against one another. "Let's do this shit," he rumbled. "I need some exercise. It's been a while."

Myna raised her arms and slowly drew a few deep

breaths. "Are we all prepared? After my conversation with Mr. Arain, I can open the portal on the edge of the illusion."

The team all nodded, their expressions fixed and serious.

The ancient Drow made a few quick movements with her hand. Her jaw tightened and she dragged in a few more deep breaths as a swirling portal grew before them. The front lawn of a wide white mansion lay on the other side of the gateway.

Alison focused her thoughts. "It's time to teach the dark wizards a lesson." She stepped through with her dad and Mason close behind. Drysi followed, then Lily. Hana was next and Myna brought up the rear a split-second before the portal snapped closed.

Pain lined the old Drow's face more than usual. She frowned and raised her hands and a dark nimbus surrounded her.

It's her choice, and I have to respect it.

Heavy magic filled the air, so thick they could practically taste it. They were obviously at the edge of the illusion.

They never told us about illusions on this scale back at the School of Necessary Magic.

The leader nodded to Lily. "Do it. They know we're here by now, so seal them in."

The half-elf held the top in her palm and traced her finger along the rim as she muttered an incantation in ancient Akkadian. A bright emerald light enveloped the artifact and it began to spin and floated from her hand.

"We're on the clock," she announced. "We'd better move."

The border of the illusion was obvious as the team jogged forward and passed through it. The air shimmered for a moment, and the empty lawn was replaced by a dozen men who raced toward them with automatic rifles.

"Should we give them a cha—" Alison began as her merciful instincts kicked in.

The defenders immediately opened fire. Their bullets bounced off the armor and shields of the strike team with no effect.

"Not anti-magic, huh? Okay, that answers that." She crouched and coiled shadow magic around her legs. "Some people simply don't like to talk."

Lily, Drysi, and Mason all returned the attack with methodical brutality. Their bullets ripped through the men with ease and left them dead on the lawn in seconds. Izzie eliminated a couple with bright white blasts.

The Welsh witch sighed. "I think I wasted your money, Alison, on poor bastards who weren't even dark wizards. I didn't bother to bring regular rounds."

Alison released the energy she'd been building and shook her head. "This must be the normal security they use in case some random cop shows up and they don't want to rouse their suspicion."

Several men with wands barreled through the front door. A thick cerulean wall pulsed directly ahead of them. Lines of similar-toned energy flowed from the wands of three of the wizards to the barrier. One of the men's wands was tucked into the front of his slacks, and he carried a black-lidded ceramic jar with both arms.

Izzie narrowed her eyes and scowled as she gestured to the artifact. "I don't like the look of that jar."

The Brownstone team members renewed their assault. Their bullets slowed as they passed through the wall and simply dropped on the other side.

"Oh, nice trick," Alison muttered sarcastically. "Dad? Do you mind clearing them out?"

James grunted and raised his arm. Green sparks erupted from both his blades and grew in density and brightness for several seconds. Massive green beams burst from the front of the blades to rocket through the shield with ease. Two of the wizards had no time to scream before the radiation punctured their chest and vaporized their lungs.

The man with the jar hauled the lid off and shouted something in a language Alison didn't recognize. Her father swept his arms in opposite directions and the motion delivered a blade-like effect that sliced the other wizards in half. The jar-bearer managed to live for a couple more seconds before his head disappeared.

The momentum of the attack continued to the house and savaged a path through the walls.

Hana laughed in delight. "Take that, assholes."

Mason shook his head, slight disbelief on his face.

"Whoa," Alison shouted. "Back it up, Dad. We need to be able to get in there to make sure we actually finish them off."

James ceased the attack but seemed disappointed. The vast front foyer and great room beyond lay partially exposed by the wide new openings carved by the powerful beams. Dozens of witches and wizards in robes stood inside, their wands at the ready. Several bodies sprawled at their feet. The defenders backed away and retreated from the great room to deeper within the mansion.

The Brownstone leader hissed as a massive pulse of magic surged near the front of the house. "What the hell was that?"

"Trouble," Izzie suggested.

The team all exchanged concerned glances.

Balls of black flame spewed violently from the jar and exploded several yards into the air to generate more black fireballs. These fell and writhed, pulsed, and jerked as if alive. The flames began to grow rather than set anything ablaze.

Myna scowled. "This will be trouble. I've seen this kind of thing before."

"What is it?" Alison asked.

"Think of it as a storage jar," the old Drow explained. "Except it stores creatures."

Some of the larger flames died out and were replaced by twelve gleaming, white-eyed horrors with dark leathery skin and twelve legs, each the size of a small horse. Razor-sharp teeth filled their massive jaws, which dripped with a viscous green liquid that seared the grass when it fell.

Additional monsters appeared from the flames and the jar continued to spit more black fireballs.

James raised a single arm this time and released a vivid green blast of energy. The missile struck an invader's head and shattered it in a shower of bright green blood. The body twitched and collapsed but the other beasts surged into the attack.

"They're not so fucking tough," he rumbled and delivered a few well-placed strikes to kill more of the creatures. They died with a loud squeal that created no distraction at all for the horde.

Alison and Izzie flung several light bolts. An exploding knife from Drysi dismembered two of the monsters into a messy pile of body parts. Hana, Lily, and Mason's bullets found their targets, but it took several slugs directly in the head to actually kill the monsters.

The small amount of pride in Alison vanished when she realized that the artifact's speed of release had actually increased. Two creatures now appeared for every single one they destroyed.

"This is fucking tedious," she yelled and sliced through an adversary with a launched shadow crescent.

"We could spend hours at this rate," Izzie agreed before she launched an exploding orb that catapulted several of their opponents' bodies into free-flight.

"I'll blow the fucking thing," James suggested. "No source, no horde."

"No!" Myna bellowed. "Whatever you do, don't do that."

Alison looked at her in confusion. The woman hadn't made a single attack yet. Instead, she'd stared intently at the jar, her eyes narrowed.

"If you destroy it, you'll release all the stored creatures at once," the old Drow explained.

"How many can it possibly hold, even with magic?" Hana asked while she ejected a magazine and reloaded.

"Who knows? It's not a portal in a true sense, but it can store things almost as if they are in another place." Myna shook her head. "There could be thousands in there.

Maybe even more, especially if they are capable of breeding without special help."

They continued to fall to the strike team's attacks, but their net population grew relentlessly.

"Shit," Alison protested. "We're too damned close to the city. If they constantly spill out like that, people will get hurt. Sure, the police can railgun these things or bomb them, but will they be able to stop thousands of giant monster bugs before they eat someone? Tahir, are you there?"

"I am," he replied through her receiver.

"Get ready to send a warning to the police and military," she ordered.

James grunted and eradicated another aggressor. "How do we stop it?"

Myna sighed. "I think I can perform a binding ritual, but it will take time."

He lurched forward and fired several quick shots and their adversaries flowed toward him. One leapt on him, and he sliced cleanly through it with his blade before he decapitated another one.

"I'll keep them busy," he yelled. "Myna can do her thing. The rest of you fucking get inside. We're on the clock."

Izzie nodded, grim-faced. "He's right. If we don't stop the leaders, it doesn't matter how many monsters or lackeys we kill."

One of the beasts finally managed to bite James with its acid-covered teeth but with no penetration and no burns. He impaled its head on a blade before he punted it away several yards, leaving a trail of bright green blood.

"I have this shit," he roared. "Hurry up."

"Okay, Tahir, hold off on the authorities," Alison ordered. "We're going in."

Myna raised her arms and closed her eyes as she began her chant. Glyphs of wispy shadow appeared in the air in front of her. "Go, my princess."

Alison, with Izzie at her side, raced toward the house and angled away from the swarm that tried to overwhelm her armored father. Lily, Drysi, Mason, and Hana fell in behind her and continued to fire at the creatures when they could.

I'm glad I brought Dad, but this isn't over yet.

CHAPTER TWENTY-ONE

The strike team surged into the foyer as the squeal of dying monsters filled the air behind them. The horde her father single-handedly suppressed served as proof of the importance of their mission and the callousness of the Seventh Order.

The jar was as dangerous as a Mountain Strider, and the order deployed it without thought of the consequences for anyone else.

I could never have imagined they would do something so dangerous. They have to be stopped. It's only a matter of time before they destroy a city.

The bodies in the foyer and great room—victims of James' earlier attack—slowed their progress until they cleared the otherwise empty rooms and entered a wide hallway. Their quick pace brought them to wide double doors.

Lily's eyes glazed for a second, and she threw a hand up. "Stop."

They skidded to a halt and waited for her explanation.

"They're ready for us?" Alison suggested. "I wasn't sure if they were simply scared of my dad or if they had some preplanned fallback position."

Hana laughed as she drew her sword. "Being ready and being able to win are two separate things." She swung her sword a few times, her expression smug. "If they were confident, they would have stood their ground."

Izzie gritted her teeth. "We can take them. Let's go in already."

Lily frowned and shook her head. "The door's trapped with a weird spell that would have locked us down in crystal. A large group of Seventh Order defenders is on the other side, from what I could see in my vision. I think they're guarding a stairwell in the back, but I couldn't see much past the point where the crystal spell activated."

Drysi snorted. "Conrad and those bloody bastards must be downstairs. I wonder if they're already trying to run. We need to hurry. Lily's artifact won't last forever."

"You're right." Mason frowned. "Depending on what kind of spells they use, they could stall us for a while. They might already have tried to portal out and realized something is blocking them. Now, they're trying to run out the clock, or they're depending on their jar monsters to overwhelm us. They might have some kind of kill switch."

Alison exhaled sharply and backed away from the door. "The Canadian government will need to retrieve that thing after Myna shuts it off and we finish this shit." She pointed at the door. "Based on your vision, Lily, where are the stairs in relation to the doors?"

Her friend gestured toward the doors. "Straight ahead. The room itself is weird. It's a massive room, but empty, with glyphs on the walls."

"It's probably a ritual chamber," she suggested. "If they've filled the room with their people, that limits what they can do."

Izzie grinned. "Are you thinking what I'm thinking, Alison?"

"Yeah." She gestured everyone back. "I'll blow straight through. It'll be more surprising that way. Hana, Mason, and Lily, do you think you could keep the wizards busy while Izzie, Drysi, and I head for the stairs?"

The fox scoffed. "I could probably take all of them on my own, and with Lily and Mason, it's practically a vacation."

The Gray Elf chuckled. "It's more that I have you two with me."

Hana winked. "Maybe we can have a little competition to see how many we take down."

Mason's grunt reminded Alison briefly of her dad. "Let's do this."

Alison channeled magical energy into an explosive orb for several seconds. The power crackled and buzzed in the otherwise quiet hallway, the sounds of the front lawn battle now distant. "On my mark. Three…"

Her friends all took deep breaths and raised their weapons.

"Two…"

We're close now. Very close.

"One…mark." She hurled the orb toward the wall.

The explosion demolished the barrier and several screams sounded, followed by thuds as bodies dropped.

This is why you don't only protect the door, idiots, and you stay away from the walls.

Hana rocketed through the smoke and burning debris as conjured fireballs, energy blasts, and even ropes careened toward the hole. She took a few strikes, but her red shield only dimmed slightly.

The huge room was filled with a throng of angry wizards and witches, but that also provided a rich target environment. The fox's movement blurred as she slashed the throat of a nearby wizard and spun to stab another, the anti-magic properties of the sword as strong as ever.

Lily and Mason were close behind her. The Gray Elf emptied her magazine into a huddle of wizards on the other side of the room and the arrogant smirks on their faces vanished as the anti-magic bullets destroyed their weak shields. The ordnance was slowed enough to save the men from instant death, but most of her targets were sufficiently wounded to make them fall.

The life wizard bulldozed into a group on the side and his punches and kicks launched them into one another. His fists flashed with each blow, a spell Alison didn't see him use often. He rapidly demolished the shields of his first couple of victims before he delivered the coup de gras on each one.

Drysi delivered rapid but measured shots as she swept the room from left to right and made sure not to aim close to any of the Brownstone team. When her gun clicked empty, she drew a red glowing dagger and hurled it into a dense group of wizards in the center of the room. The explosion scorched the floor and scattered the enemies. A few of the men survived and seemed virtually untouched. They had better shields than some of their associates, perhaps. The not so lucky remainder, burned and bleeding, sprawled around them.

Side doors opened, and more magical defenders flooded in, along with men with rifles. The Welshwoman killed four of the riflemen with a single explosive dagger.

Alison swung to pepper the center of the room with a steady stream of shadow crescents that swept a handful of their adversaries to their doom.

They really are making their last stand here.

She extended a shadow blade and stabbed and slashed viciously at anyone in her path as she rushed toward the stairs. "This has to be most of the Seventh Order. We'll crush their army and leaders at the same time."

A brave wizard conjured a glowing rapier out of thin air. She carved through it and continued the smooth motion to stab him in the heart.

Izzie pivoted and flung bright blasts in different directions to wound and kill the foot soldiers of the Seventh Order. Unlike Lily and Hana, who both looked like they were actually having a good time, her expression remained a grim mask of determination.

This isn't only about the occasional attack for her. This is about getting her life back and freeing both her and her mom. We have to win here and now for both of them.

Lily ejected her magazine and transferred her pistol into her other hand. She drew her magic dagger and cartwheeled behind two wizards before she stabbed both in the back of the neck. A quick twist of her body saved her from an ice spear that plunged into a nearby enemy instead.

Angry shouts and chaos gripped the room now, with the Seventh Order army clearly unable to focus on who presented the most important target. Whatever strategy they might have had crumbled beneath the relentless assault of the Brownstone strike team.

A few groups of defenders backed into the corners of the room. They took advantage of the many men and women ahead of them who served as de facto meat shields. The extra time enabled them to fold the nearby walls around them into makeshift wooden castles from which they deployed their wands through narrow murder holes.

Mason's fist flashed as he hammered it into a wizard with a crunch that indicated bones breaking. The target collapsed, clutched his chest, and groaned in pain.

"You don't have time to mess around here, A," the life wizard shouted. "Go!"

Drysi threw another knife into the center of the room and followed this rapidly with another toward one of the corner castles. The first explosion cleared a small path toward the stairs, and the second set the wooden haven on fire.

Hana shoved toward the center as she hacked and swung on one side of the group. Lily reloaded and alternated between shots and bold swipes with her enchanted dagger. Mason focused more on disrupting the enemy with quick punches. He darted in, delivered a few blows, and withdrew before the enemy could regroup.

Izzie sprinted toward the stairs, taking advantage of Drysi's opening and the way the others drew the focus of the enemy. Alison raced after her, and the Welsh witch hurled another blade at a corner castle before she followed.

A wizard raised his wand to attack but Alison cut through it and his arm with her shadow blade. He screamed and fell back, and the witch eliminated him with a shot to the head.

"I'm burning through these anti-magic bullets," the Welsh witch announced as they reached the top of the spiral stone staircase. She ejected the magazine, reloaded, and holstered the weapon before she drew two more knives. "And these are more fun anyway."

They took a few steps down.

Alison and Izzie both thrust magic bolts toward the top of the stairs as a few of the defenders attempted to pursue them. The appearance of a gleeful Hana who swung her *tachi* wildly, her tails swaying with the same exuberance, ended the dark wizard attempt.

Izzie vaulted onto the curved stone wall and the bottom of her feet glowed as she ran down the side. Drysi continued down the stairs with wide strides that allowed her to take multiple stairs at once. Alison launched upward and grew shadow wings.

She narrowed her eyes. The screams and explosions from above them had already grown distant, and it was hard to ignore the sensation that emanated from the building beneath them. It explained why the Seventh Order army had decided to make their stand above.

Dad and Myna will take care of those monsters. Hana, Lily, and Mason can handle those bastards above, but all of this is pointless if we don't destroy the four leaders. They have to be below.

"Do you feel that?" she asked.

"Yes, strong magic," Izzie replied. "Very strong magic. And these aren't exactly standard basement stairs."

Drysi smiled, but it didn't reach her eyes. "It's time for us to say hello and goodbye to Conrad and his mates."

CHAPTER TWENTY-TWO

By the time they reached the bottom of the stairs, they'd descended so far that they could barely make out the sounds of the battle above. An occasional scream or explosion would echo down to at least remind them that it still raged.

Massive glyphs covered a huge iron door immediately ahead.

We need to hurry. My team can handle it, but the longer we delay this, the more chance the leaders might have to somehow bring in reinforcements.

"I don't think we can blow through this one," Izzie muttered. "We'll have to do this the annoying way."

Alison raised her hands and nodded. "We can counter the wards. It feels like they've layered them, but if we work together, it shouldn't be too difficult."

Drysi sheathed her knives and drew her wand. "I don't think this door is what we sensed. There's something else going on—something behind the door."

Their leader nodded. "Yeah, there's always still more.

First things first." She approached the barrier and placed a hand on it. Her other hand moved in a series of intricate motions as she chanted her counter-spell and fed magic into it.

Thank you, Myna, for all your help with glyph and ward training. I'm a hell of a lot better at them now than I was before I met you.

Her two companions moved forward to do the same.

A glyph faded from the surface and a ward weakened… then another, followed by another. Each gleaming light that died bolstered her spirit.

These all feel sloppy and weak. I wonder if they were upstairs when we arrived and ran down here to throw up some quick and dirty defenses.

She grinned. "We took them completely by surprise. I wondered about that because they have so many defenders here, but they obviously never suspected we would find this place."

Drysi matched her grin. "Tidy."

Izzie removed a glyph and shrugged. "Why would they? I've hunted them for years, and you hunted them for most of the last year, but it wasn't until recently that we've gotten close." She glanced at Drysi. "Mostly thanks to her lead, and as far as the Seventh Order knew, she was dead."

"I won't lie and say I had some great plan based around that," the witch explained, "but I did think it would work out better for everyone if they thought I was dead."

Alison nodded. "If they knew you were alive, they might have been more worried about what I learned from you."

The seconds ticked into minutes as they continued the

tedious process of disabling the glyphs. More of the arcane symbols died until finally, none remained. Without them to distract her, a small carving of a robed man holding a wand drew Alison's eye.

Izzie reached tentatively toward the huge brass handles in the middle of the doors, but her hesitation was momentary. The massive iron doors pulled open with a squeak. With all the magic available to the Seventh Order, they hadn't bothered to oil the hinges.

Another wide, stone-lined corridor extended before them and sloped gently down into a four-way intersection. There was no apparent light source, but the tunnels were dim rather than dark. It seemed more like the beginning of an underground complex than a maze.

The three women pushed forward, not confused for even a moment about where to go. The same heavy magic that they'd sensed before provided an easy compass.

"We might find something annoying there," Alison observed as they jogged steadily toward their destination—whatever it might be.

"It's better that we find it rather than wait for it to find us," Izzie replied.

Drysi nodded. "I agree."

"I simply want to be sure we all want the same thing."

"As long it involves a very dead Seventh Order, I'm happy," the bounty hunter snarled.

"It's almost over, Izzie. Soon, you'll be free."

The trio fell into a tense silence and focused on the way ahead.

The path turned a few times and other intersections appeared. Glyph-covered wooden doors lined the passages through the underground complex, but they ignored all of them as they continued toward the building magic they sensed.

I couldn't have done this by myself. Nor could Izzie. Even having Dad wouldn't have been enough. All my friends and allies are helping me end this shit and free Izzie.

She picked the pace up and her companions matched hers immediately. They seemed close to the source of the magic, but the end of the long, wide hallway remained cloaked in darkness. Nothing materialized from the black-swallowed corridor until they stepped into what seemed to be pure night.

In an instant, the stone was gone, along with the tunnels. Everything had vanished and a verdant field under a clear sky replaced it.

Alison frowned and shook her head. It felt too cool despite the sun shining in the sky. This was obviously another illusion. But why?

Four robed people stood in the distance, each with masks in different colors to obscure their features—black, blue, yellow, and white. They pointed their wands at the sky and energy swirled above them. A glowing, glyph-filled circle on the ground revolved slowly around them.

"I'll take a wild guess and say we found the leaders of the Seventh Order," she said after a moment of silence in which they all gathered their wits.

The four magicals lowered their wands and focused on the strike team. Their masks effectively concealed their expressions. The glowing circle faded, and the field vanished to be replaced by a vast stone chamber. Densely packed complicated glyphs filled the walls and ceiling, but the floor remained untouched by anything except dust and time.

The black-masked figure scoffed derisively. "Jones," he hissed in a clear English accent. "Your presence here with them explains so much, you traitor. I knew I should have killed you long ago, but perhaps this is still salvageable."

Drysi pointed at him. "That's Conrad."

The blue-masked figure chuckled. "I'm Tabitha." She pointed to the yellow-masked figure. "Jeanne." A final gesture indicated the white-masked figure, who was visibly larger than any of the others. "Zachariah."

Alison frowned. "Why so friendly all of a sudden?"

"You should know who it is that kills you," Conrad replied. "But perhaps it doesn't have to come to that. The fact that you are here is a testimony to your power, and power can be very stabilizing when guided properly. We never had to be enemies. Quite frankly, we still don't, provided certain behavioral changes are implemented."

Izzie barked a scornful laugh. "Are you fucking kidding me? You want to negotiate now? After all these years—including screwing with me when I was still a kid?" She gestured behind her, although currently, there was nothing there but the large open doors. "Your entire army is being slaughtered upstairs and outside. Your doomsday jar? Some centuries-old Drow and James Brownstone are handling it. The only reason we're not up there to help them finish everything off is because we were worried you would run if we took too long."

The wizard sighed and shook his head. "You shouldn't interfere. Don't you understand that? All we're doing is returning the world to its proper order—something nature herself is doing, albeit slowly. If man is good at anything, it's improving on nature." He held a gloved hand up. "Today's ritual was nothing dangerous. Merely preparation for something more important in the near future. If you savages would calm yourself for a few minutes, you might understand that you could also come to benefit from what we're about to do. The violence can end. We can be allies."

Alison made no effort to hide her contempt. "You've tried to kidnap Izzie for most of her life, and now, you want to cut a deal? I don't know if I can roll my eyes hard enough to account for how stupid this sounds."

Conrad waved a dismissive hand. "Because her Fixer father would never understand, but she's seen the truth of the world—the cruelty and the chaos. So have you, Alison Brownstone. You know this world is sick, and we can fix it. Leaving it as it is means condemning people to unnecessary suffering. Don't delude yourself. That is a moral choice as well."

"You'll save people by killing innocents?" Drysi asked incredulously.

His head swiveled toward her and he didn't respond for several seconds. "You're pathetic, Jones. This is why your family deserves to fall into disrepute and poverty. You're a traitor to your family and our greater ideals. You're myopic and more concerned with your feelings than your duty."

"It's a valid question, Barnes," Alison interjected. "I've seen many dark wizards kill people, including your own people, so I need to understand what makes you different."

He shrugged. "We've made mistakes. I'll admit that, but I can assure you it was all for the greater good."

"Releasing the Mountain Strider was for the greater

good?" She raised a skeptical eyebrow. "If I hadn't stopped it, that monster could have killed numerous people and it still did a lot of damage."

"You misunderstood, Miss Brownstone." Conrad tapped his wand in his palm. "We've never sought your destruction. You interfered with our plans and you forced our hand in that regard. Yes, we've sought Izzie..." He paused and might have looked behind them, but his eyes remained hidden. "Your parents aren't here, are they, Miss Berens?"

"No," Izzie replied, her voice flat. "They're helping out an old friend. Don't worry. I'm more than enough Berens for you. I'll share your dying words, though."

Drysi held her hands near her vest and her remaining knives. "I was supposed to be more in the know than most, and you still never told me the complete bloody plan. Everything you had me do seemed to end in death."

"Go ahead, Conrad," Jeanne interrupted. A French accent defined her voice. "Tell them. They either join us now, or they die. It doesn't hurt for them to know."

Alison frowned as her mind raced. The leaders of the Seventh Order might be stalling, but if they were about to explain what the hell it was they had been doing, that could be helpful.

You assholes assume you can win? Bad bet, but you'll see that soon enough.

Conrad raised his wand. Alison and Izzie both raised their hands in response. Drysi yanked out a dagger.

"Oh, there's no need for violence," he assured them with the trace of a smile in his words. "Not yet, anyway." He turned and waved the wand.

An image of Earth appeared with dots across the surface.

"There are a small number of magical pressure points between Earth and Oriceran throughout the world. Places, you see, where magic flows slightly differently." The globe rotated and zoomed in on Washington state. A dot appeared where Seattle lay.

"They aren't immediately obvious," Conrad continued, "because of ancient wards—ones so old they were created before the last time the gates opened, maybe even before two openings ago. They regulate the magical pressure, in a way. One theory suggests that they are much like valves put in place by the ancients. We call them the Great Pillars, and our research suggests that they are linked to the gates. There is a narrow window after the beginning of the opening of the gates in which these Great Pillars can be manipulated. This might be why so few magicals know about them."

Alison frowned. "I've never heard of this before. Don't you think it would be common knowledge?"

The wizard scoffed. "Why? So many are ignorant, even the ancient Oricerans. They fall into easy patterns and forget their true power. Hiding magic has allowed secrets to remain, even hidden from the most ancient of gnomes."

Izzie gestured toward the globe. "What the hell does this have to do with me and my mom?"

"You have a unique access to power. We became aware of it years ago. Activating a Great Pillar would be easier with your help and ritual access to the power of your line." He shrugged. "It's as simple as that, Miss Berens. There are few other individuals we're aware of who provide such easy access to power that we can concentrate for our purposes."

"You need us as glorified keys?" The bounty hunter's face scrunched in disgust. "So you can snatch more power? That's why you took my life from me?"

Conrad sighed. "Don't be so melodramatic. We didn't do anything. The Fixer is simply short-sighted. You have to understand the potential. Imagine having the ability to call on magic as if the gates were fully open, but to do that right now on Earth instead of waiting for thousands of years. We can't force a gate through a Great Pillar, but we can gain access to the power as if it were already open. This will allow us to attain our rightful place, but it can be shared with those with the same vision. We can make our chosen few much, much stronger than other magicals so they can assume their rightful rule."

Alison stared at the man and allowed all her anger and frustration to suffuse her face. "You were prepared to kill hundreds, if not thousands, of people in Seattle with the Mountain Strider, and that's not even your main plan. I suspect this Great Pillar plan ends up with—oh, I get it." She snapped her fingers. "There's something in particular about Seattle. There's a Great Pillar there that's easy to get to or..." She narrowed her eyes. "Is that why the Galbrathians blew up the kemana?"

"All great causes require great sacrifice," Conrad declared. "Steps had to be taken, and the Galbrathians proved a useful tool for us in that particular regard, even if their own goals were far more vicious and nihilist in fundamental motivation."

"Do you have any idea how many people died there?"

she shouted. "My friend's parents died. Have you seen what's it's like down there? Moments are burned into time. Ghosts that aren't ghosts. It's…wrong."

"Everyone dies, Miss Brownstone," he replied in a bored tone. "But if you want fewer deaths in the long run, your best chance is to support us. We'll bring order to this world exactly as it was accomplished on Oriceran. Their planet isn't ruled by a president or prime minister selected through some meaningless election, but by a king. Their Great Treaty only works because of the power wielded by the greatest beings on a world already saturated with magic. We'll simply accelerate the process on Earth and ensure that the right types of magicals have that power and authority. Everything will be as it should."

Alison laughed. "You actually believe that bullshit, don't you?"

"Savage children to the end. Unfortunate."

"I've been called worse." Drysi shrugged, her expression hard.

Izzie glared at him. "I want my life back, but you can't give that to me, so I'll simply kill you instead."

"I won't even give you one chance, Barnes." Alison extended a shadow blade. "The last thing this planet needs is a group of assholes who kill people to gain more power. We'll end this fucking farce, and you'll pay for everyone your plans have killed."

Conrad sighed. "A pity." He stepped back and raised his wand. "You'll find, Miss Brownstone, that there's a reason why we lead the Seventh Order. And don't think, Miss Berens, that we can't hurt you. We merely can't kill you."

CHAPTER TWENTY-THREE

Drysi threw two daggers while the other two women both fired blasts of light magic at the wizard. All the attacks exploded against an invisible shield halfway between the strike team and the four Seventh Order leaders.

Conrad sneered and shook his head. "You were fools to come here. No matter what happens, we will ensure that you never leave this place."

The four masked magicals raised their wands and chanted. Rough stone men ripped themselves from the walls to create huge holes and clouds of dust.

"Okay, that's annoying," Alison muttered.

The Welsh witch obliterated one of the conjured stone warriors with a well-thrown dagger and small chunks pinwheeled from the destruction. Alison and Izzie charged their attacks before they released explosive orbs into other stone men. The missiles pulverized the creations, but more and more emerged from the walls.

"You really like your cannon fodder," Alison called. She

glanced at Conrad and the others, who held their previous positions and continued their chant.

Izzie rushed to Alison's side. "Do you notice how they don't do anything else?" she murmured.

"The shield isn't one-way. I'll test it and look for a weak point. Keep destroying their new friends." Alison grew shadow wings and elevated until she was only a few feet below the high ceiling. She flung a few different attacks—light orbs, light bolts, and shadow crescents—toward their enemies, only for the order's shield to stop it. "All the way to the top, huh?"

Izzie maintained her assaults and spun and whirled as she worked methodically to demolish the seemingly endless waves of statues.

Drysi gritted her teeth. "We'll lose if we try to win a bloody attrition fight." She drew her wand and started a quick, complicated incantation in Welsh.

Conrad laughed, while the others continued the chant. "Even if you can win, Brownstone, you can't kill us without dooming Vancouver. The Jar of the Hungry has already been opened above the city. By the time you learn how to close it, those creatures will have been released everywhere. They are naturally attracted to souls. If you care so much about saving lives, you should surrender immediately. I can reverse the jar and contain all those beasts."

Alison snorted. "That's your big backup plan? Holding a city hostage? Don't worry, I have my dad and a really cranky ancient Drow handling that." She extended a shadow blade and slashed at the shield, but nothing she'd attempted thus far seemed to penetrate. "And if the power of James Brownstone and the wisdom of Myna can't solve a problem, nothing can."

The wizard simply scoffed and nodded at Tabitha. "It's time."

She stopped chanting and the two leaders took several steps back and began a complicated series of wand motions and a sinister-sounding incantation Alison didn't understand.

They should give Professor Powell a raise at the School of Necessary Magic. Even trying to remotely prepare students to face this is hard. Working bounties helped me but knowing the kind of crap dark wizards might pull is damned helpful, too.

Drysi shouted the end of her own incantation. A bright halo of dark-blue energy surrounded her body, and her hair drifted upward as if she floated in water. Blood leaked from her mouth and eyes.

"What are you doing?" Alison called, more than a little concerned at the transformation.

The Welsh witch ignored her and turned toward her former leaders, hatred in her eyes.

Izzie frowned and continued her battle with the armed men. Piles of broken, rough stone limbs and dust now filled their side of the room. Most of the nearby walls were gone and long tunnels had formed, but new stone warriors advanced constantly, the product of Zachariah and Jeanne's continued efforts.

Alison flew back, her hands out, and funneled light and shadow magic into an orb in front of her. They needed to get through the shield to even have a chance to finish the fight. She had no idea what Drysi intended, but it didn't matter if they couldn't deliver a single strike to their adversaries.

"*Y dechrau a'r diwedd!*" the witch shouted, her wand pointed forward. Three bright blue orbs appeared near the tip, converged and flared, and grew to form a long, thin energy spear. She screamed, and the weapon careened forward.

It exploded against the invisible shield in a shower of flames that quickly spread across the middle of the room to form a curtain of blue fire that separated the two forces. Conrad and Tabitha ignored it and continued their spell.

Huh. Okay, then.

As if she hadn't even noticed the attack, Izzie summoned two bright light whips. She cracked through two stone men approaching her, split them in half, and ended their short new existence. Another rapid attack destroyed two others.

Drysi dropped to her hands and knees and coughed blood. "Shield…coming…down."

The blue flame faded to reveal Zachariah pointing his wand at the witch.

"Look out!" Alison shouted

The wizard conjured and launched a barbed black arrow that spun toward his target. The half-Drow plummeted toward the arrow in a feeble attempt to intercept it.

Drysi scrambled to her feet as if to try to avoid it, but the arrow pierced her chest and her shield disappeared. She cried out in pain as the momentum of the magical projectile carried her body into a nearby wall. The arrow embedded itself several inches deep in the stone.

"I won't… lie… That…fucking…hurts." She coughed and spat more blood before her head slumped forward.

Damn it.

Alison landed and released her wings. She ran toward the woman. A black arrow narrowly missed her, and she replied with a few light blasts of her own. Zachariah's shield absorbed the strikes, but he winced and stumbled back.

A sword of flame surrounded Jeanne's wand. Fire leapt from the sword and surrounded her entire body but didn't consume or burn her. She bellowed a challenge and charged Izzie.

Huh. Tired of playing with statues?

Conrad and Tabitha continued their ritual. Bright lines appeared on the ceiling and glyphs winked into existence on the floor.

Shit. I need to get to Drysi.

The witch hung on the wall, not moving, and her blood dripped steadily.

Alison continued her race and Zachariah's next attack caught her in the shoulder. Pain exploded through her body. The arrow hurtled her forward, but she gritted her teeth and yanked hard to remove it before she impacted with a wall or an exposed rockface. She released the projectile and fell to roll a few times. The arrow continued without her until it buried itself deep into the wall.

Another instinctive roll saved her from the next arrow, and two follow-up explosive orbs forced her attacker back. Her shoulder throbbed, but she ignored the pain. Drysi was in a lot worse shape.

Izzie finished the last of the stone men, which gave

Jeanne time to move closer, her sword of pure flame held aloft.

"You assholes made my life a living hell because you wanted a battery for your twisted plan?" Izzie shouted. She cracked her light whips at her approaching adversary.

The witch hissed as the attacks sliced through her shield and into her flesh. She stumbled back and her flame aura weakened.

"If you'd left me alone, I would probably have never come after you," the bounty hunter continued. One of the whips disappeared, and the other brightened intensely. "But you could never be satisfied." Her laugh was harsh and humorless. "Didn't you ever think the implications through? The same reason you want me is the same reason you should never have tried to take me on. You might have had a chance when I didn't have memories and was a kid, but no more. It's been years, and you've never been able to capture me."

She strode forward and the whip flared to become blindingly bright. "All that power I can call on. All the power of my entire line. I almost never need to use it because it's dangerous if it's out of control, but sometimes, a woman has to make a point."

Alison darted toward Zachariah while she propelled a steady stream of rapid blasts to distract him with one hand and shoved more magic into her shadow blade in the another. The wizard managed a few more arrows, but she dodged those easily with quick air bursts.

The glyphs grew denser around Conrad and Tabitha. She didn't know what they were doing and didn't dare take the time to try to examine the magic in detail.

Jeanne shrank back from the bounty hunter, whose body was now surrounded by a bright nimbus.

"You don't have enough experience to control that much power," Jeanne cried.

"Neither do you!" Izzie yelled. "This is for all the years you bastards took from me." She cracked the whip and the tip struck her opponent. A blinding pulse incinerated the witch and left only burning fragments of cloth and the scorched yellow mask that clattered to the floor and split in half.

One down, Alison thought.

She managed to close on the backpedaling wizard. He launched another arrow, and she sliced it in half with her shadow blade before doing the same to him.

Alison spun to face the two remaining leaders of the Seventh Order.

Izzie marched toward Conrad and Tabitha. "Your turn."

The half-Drow paused and looked from the wizards to Drysi before she released her shadow blade and sprinted toward the wounded witch.

The dark wizards ceased their chant.

"You can't win," Conrad explained, his voice still completely calm. "If you kill us, this entire complex will collapse. This is what will happen. You will end whatever spell is blocking our portals, and you will allow us to leave. You can take some pride in a partial victory, little Berens and Brownstone, but this doesn't end. I'll admit you've wounded the order today, but in some ways, you've done me a favor. Those two always were…troublesome. Without them, our planning will be more efficient."

"This building will collapse?" Izzie stopped, instantly

alert. "Alison, are you thinking what I'm thinking?" A vicious grin appeared on her face.

Let's see. What could... Oh, yeah, let's do this Hollingsworth style.

"Probably. Give me one second." She reached Drysi, yanked the arrow out of the wounded witch, and caught her before she fell.

Thank goodness. She's still breathing.

She retrieved a healing potion, poured it down her throat, and followed up with a hasty awakening spell.

The woman hissed as her eyes fluttered open. "I have the bloody Devil's own luck." Her wounds had already begun to heal.

The half-Drow cast a healing spell on her own shoulder before she helped her companion to her feet.

Izzie stood a few yards away from Conrad and Tabitha, a satisfied look on her face.

"Stay close," Alison murmured to Drysi. "And I'll keep you alive." She jogged toward her friend and grew shadow wings. With a deep breath, she summoned two purple-black shadow tendrils, something she'd worked on with Myna but still needed practice with.

It doesn't have to be fancy, merely to work.

The Welshwoman wiped the blood off her mouth, her expression one of hatred and disgust. "Oh, Conrad, you're the worst kind of fucker, and I'll enjoy seeing you die, especially since you're such a smug git."

"Don't worry, Jones." he sneered in response. "Perhaps I'll have to realign our plans to avoid Berens, but I assure you, I will find you and kill you, no matter what pathetic hovel you crawl into as befitting your fallen family."

Tabitha offered a mocking smile in agreement but remained silent.

Alison channeled magical energy into her wings, tendrils, and legs. "I'm ready, Izzie, whenever you are."

Conrad snorted. "Aren't you listening, Brownstone? This entire complex will collapse. You're powerful, but can you survive being buried under so many tons of dirt and stone? Are you desperate enough to trade your lives for ours? I can see the pathetic witch feeling that way and maybe even Berens, but you?"

"Who said anything about trading our lives?" She grinned. "Do it, Izzie."

"This is for my mom." The bounty hunter's whip incinerated Tabitha first. The wizard's eyes widened in disbelief as she raised her arm once more. "And this is for me."

"You're insane," he screamed a moment before she obliterated him.

The glyphs on the ceiling and floor surged with bright light and massive cracks ripped through the stone above them.

Izzie groaned and stumbled forward, and the whip vanished. "Maybe...I...overdid it. Only a little."

Drysi looked up as huge chunks of stone fell from the ceiling. "At least Conrad's dead," she muttered with what sounded like false cheer.

"Don't freak," Alison ordered. Her shadow tendrils wound around the two women and raised them both.

"Bloody hell," the Welsh witch shouted.

The half-Drow released the energy in her legs and launched herself into a rapid retreat, mere feet off the floor, out of the chamber with her teammates safely encircled in the magic tendrils. Drysi yelped with excitement.

If those Hollingsworth assholes can use thrustpacks inside, I can get away with some shadow wings and a few passengers.

She concentrated to make quick turns and avoid the collapsing structure as she flew back to the stairs. The rest of the world faded away, and she barely even remembered that she carried the other two women until they arrived at the stairway. Without hesitation, she traveled upward, her flight path spiraling with the structure.

They burst from the stairwell a few seconds before rubble filled it. The entire mansion shuddered. The walls cracked, and it was obvious that not only the underground chambers would be destroyed.

Dead bodies littered the floor, and she tried to ignore them as she focused on the flight toward the front of the building. Once or twice, she gave in to temptation and chanced a hurried glance in search of her other team members. She didn't see them, but her search hadn't been anywhere near thorough. Hopefully, they hadn't fallen in the carnage.

Alison lowered her head and raised her passengers level with her body as she aimed for one of the holes her father's earlier attack had created. Seconds after they soared out of the mansion, the entire structure collapsed in on itself.

CHAPTER TWENTY-FOUR

Alison spun and released her friends, who landed on the grass with soft grunts. Loud shouts and shrieks drew her attention to the enormous piles of dead monsters that filled the lawn. Swarms of living creatures streamed from the jar, oblivious to the dead.

Several careened wildly when James threw them off. He spun and slashed into several others that tried to overrun him. From what she could see, the invaders were focused on her dad and Myna.

Relief flowed through her at the sight of Mason, Hana, and Lily near her mentor. The old Drow stood firm and continued to chant as if oblivious to the horde that bore down on her. Dark streams of shadows flowed over her body, and strong magic pulsed from her.

The Gray Elf slashed and stabbed viciously with her dagger, her movements quick and graceful and almost a dance as she eliminated the enemy systematically. A cartwheel brought her face-to-face with another, and she thrust a knife through its head before she spun to slash the stomach of the next. She hadn't escaped either the house or the lawn without injury, though. A few burns marred her back, and blood seeped from a large, jagged slash in her side.

Hana hacked away with her *tachi*, her skin almost back to its normal color. The blade carved into the stream of attackers with ease to send them shrieking and howling into death. Blood coated her blade, and her vulpine eyes remained watchful for the approaching enemy.

Mason stood the closest to Myna. His purpose seemed to be to punch and kick aside the killers that targeted her and set them up as easy targets for Lily and Hana. Occasionally, he drew his gun and fired a few decisive shots.

Alison released her wings and settled on the ground before she fired a stream of light bolts into the monsters. They collapsed under the attack and their flesh sizzled. Fatigue clawed at the edge of her mind, but everyone needed to do their part to give the old Drow more time to complete the spell.

Even if these beasts were easy for an elite team of security consultants and bounty hunters to slay, the average human in Vancouver wouldn't have enchanted swords or powerful magic to defend them.

James bellowed with rage and leapt forward to land in the middle of a patch of black flames that were in the process of transformation. He hacked into the blaze to dissipate them and kill some of the emerging creatures before they could even form. There were now so many fire nurseries that even the direct front-line assault of the

Extended Advanced James Brownstone couldn't stem the tide of killers that spilled past him and converged on Myna, the slavering jaws eager to close around the Drow.

It didn't matter who else might kill them. The invaders seemed to sense the threat she represented.

Izzie stood, swaying on her feet. "Damn it." She raised her arm, fired a bolt, and felled another creature. "I didn't go through all of that shit to lose now to some damned monster horde."

Drysi raised her wand and managed a fireball, but it took a couple to eliminate her target. "I wish I had a few explosive knives left."

Despite the huge numbers they faced, the mounds of corpses funneled the new arrivals into kill zones that bene- fitted the Brownstone team, but it was obvious they couldn't eliminate them fast enough. It was only a matter of time before they were overwhelmed or some of the creatures broke off to head for the city. The mansion might be on the outskirts of Vancouver, but it wasn't in the wilderness. A horde of twelve-legged venomous killers could treat the city like her father treated All-You-Can-Eat barbecue.

"Tahir, are you there?" Alison asked as she directed a barrage of explosive orbs into the steady stream of monsters.

"I've already sent notice to the Canadians," he replied. "Police and military forces are rushing to form a defensive line in case we can't hold the monsters there. They didn't even bother to question who I was or my report once I mentioned your name and your father's. I've monitored some of their military channels, and they are also preparing to launch planes and attack helicopters."

Shit. Tahir mentioned Dad. That might get him in trouble, but making sure they're protecting Vancouver is more important. I believe in Myna, but there are so many of these damned things.

"Good job," she replied and appreciated her infomancer's instincts. She maintained her attacks, even though she wondered if an explosive orb accomplished much more than a bolt or if they were simply a waste of energy. A charged attack would take too long, though, especially given the goal of protecting Myna.

She glanced quickly at the ancient Drow. The shadows surrounding her grew thicker until they obscured her entire body.

That looks like progress, right? At least I hope it is.

James vaulted toward the old woman, and his massive leap feigned flight for a few seconds. He crushed a beast on landing, took a few seconds to charge, and fired twin beams once more. His attack incinerated dozens of the invaders and cleared the immediate threat to provide the team with a few precious seconds free from a direct attack.

A nova of thick shadow erupted from Myna and swept through the area. It didn't hurt the team or even the enemy, but when it struck the jar, the artifact wobbled and emitted a deep, loud groan. The flames froze before they retreated inside.

Alison paused and stared at the object. "Did she do it?"

The aggressors howled as black flames consumed their bodies and flowed back toward the jar. The corpses began to change form, and soon, the wobbling receptacle sucked all the reappearing black flames into itself.

She threw her arms up. "Yes! Good job, Myna." She smiled. "You lose, Conrad, you son of a bitch. I hope you're watching in hell."

Drysti and Izzie both lowered their arms, exhaustion etched into their faces.

Hana sheathed her sword with a weary smile and Mason looked at Alison with a relieved expression. "Are you okay, A?"

She nodded. "I've been better, but I'll live."

James growled and stared as the corpses around him became flames and flowed back to their source. He lowered his arms slowly, still tense as if he expected them to immediately transform back into a killer invasion.

Myna remained standing, her arms in the air as she chanted, her eyes now solid black. The intensity of the magic that poured off her had increased.

The mountains of corpses became mounds and then mere piles, and the black flame continued to swirl back into the floating receptacle.

James retracted his blades and helmet. He marched toward his daughter, a frown on his face. "Please tell me you killed those motherfuckers. That was some of the most annoying shit I've ever had to do. Those things were as tiresome as Zain."

"All four of the leaders are dead," she replied with a decisive nod. "Along with what I think is most of the people in the Seventh Order, given how many were inside the mansion." She pointed at the artifact. "Conrad made it clear that this was supposed to be their final escape plan. They intended to trade their freedom in exchange for disabling it, but they didn't know the kind of allies I had."

She beamed a smile at Myna. "Today, we won, and the Seventh Order lost badly. Completely. Sons of bitches."

The last of the bodies flamed and flowed into the jar. The lid closed on its own, and it fell with a soft thud. It was such an innocuous-looking object considering the death and destruction it contained.

James grunted. "Where's a Clown of Doom when you need one?"

"Good job, Myna."

The old Drow dropped to her knees and blood trickled from her mouth as she coughed. Her eyes returned to normal.

Alison rushed to her side and placed her hand on the woman's side to brace her. "Are you okay?"

Her mentor wheezed as she took several deep, labored breaths. "You have to understand, my princess."

"Understand what?" Her stomach knotted and her heart hammered a racing rhythm.

"Before I found you, I thought there was nothing left to live for. I'd convinced myself of that for decades. Maybe even centuries." Myna raised her head. Even though her eyes had returned to normal, blood stained her mouth, cheeks, and even her throat. "I thought all my centuries of living were a waste, a cruel joke played on me because I didn't support Laena. I kept asking myself, 'What point is there when all I am will go away, and all I was is despised by my own people?'"

Alison knelt in front of the woman and took her hands in hers. "Everything you've taught me since I've met you has made me stronger. If it wasn't for you, I wouldn't have been able to stop the Mountain Strider. Your lessons have helped me save thousands of lives and defeat enemies that I never imagined having to face. I thank you for everything you've done, and today, you probably saved thousands if not tens of thousands of people's lives." She laughed. "The Canadians will probably name a maple syrup after you. Don't worry about the portal. I'll get the Canadians to give us a ride, or we'll take a flight home or something."

Myna coughed, and her lips reddened with a new surge of blood. "The final meaning at the end of life is what's most important. It overwrites everything else that came before. I realize that now. Everything in my existence built to me finding you and instructing you, my princess. I know you think you have no place among the Drow, but I also know that's not true. I know you have a destiny with our people. A great one that will be unmatched by any who have come before you. I have no right to give you orders, but I only request that you listen in these final moments to my plea."

Hana gasped while James grunted and looked away. Izzie and Mason sighed.

Alison dragged in a deep breath and her eyes widened. "No, no, no. You have more time. You can't die yet, not after we took down all those bastards. You were critical to this operation. Without you, we wouldn't have been able to surprise them, and we wouldn't have been able to stop the jar."

Myna managed a slight laugh between wheezes. "It's too much. All the magic I used has been too much. Perhaps if the Seventh Order hadn't brought that artifact..." A spasm of coughs wracked her body. She fell forward, and Alison caught her. "Perhaps then, I might have squeezed out a few more days, but I have no regrets."

"No, it's not that." She shook her head. "You're dying because of me. You took my AMDS. You brought us here even though you knew it would hurt you, and you had to seal the jar. It was too much, and I should have insisted you not strain yourself, even if it made you hate me."

"Dying because of you?" The Drow shook her head. "No, my princess. I'm dying for you and now, as the end nears, I can die without regrets. Otherwise, I would have thought all those centuries were a waste. But now, I know they weren't, and I only know what it's like to actually live a life and not merely exist because of these few months I've spent with you."

Hana sniffled. Mason watched in complete silence, his jaw tight. Izzie released another long sigh, an apologetic look on her face. Drysi shook her head and muttered something about Conrad and hell.

"The princesses are on the move, Alison," Myna whispered. "You understand that now, and even though I'm at my end, I know you'll do what's right, not what is merely the most comfortable."

The ancient body began to fade before it transformed into a black mist and flowed into the sky. Alison tried to hug the Drow woman to her, but soon, only the dress remained. The black mist drifted upward and slowly spread.

She released the garment and stood, swallowed, and wiped away a tear. "Myna, I, Alison Brownstone, the

Princess of the Shadow Forged, recognize your sacrifice. I recognize that you perished in battle against my foes and saved many innocent people in Vancouver. You have lived a life of honor and strength, and I'll make sure all Drow speak of you with respect."

CHAPTER TWENTY-FIVE

Canadian police, emergency personnel, and military picked through the rubble of the wreckage of the mansion. They had arranged the recovered bodies and draped tarps over them.

This wasn't only a job or a raid. This was a damned war. We finally won, but not without losses.

Alison had a brief conversation with a military officer who made it clear the Canadian government would likely "find" a bounty to justify the incursion, and they also waited for proper personnel to arrive to take custody of the jar. She didn't worry much. It was doubtful that any government wanted to take on James Brownstone, his daughter, and the Fixer's daughter at the same time, along with their friends.

Drysi, Lily, and Izzie stood in the distance where they talked and gestured and offered a few details to the Canadians. Several people surrounded the still-armored James with eager looks on their faces as they asked him questions. Alison wasn't sure if they questioned him about the incident or were simply fans.

Mason rubbed her hand. "She saved a lot of people. It wasn't a waste, you know."

She sighed and nodded toward her father in the distance. "I told you about my first summer at the agency."

He nodded. "You said you were acting like a princess, and they helped toughen you up." He shook his head. "It's hard to imagine the prissy Alison who can barely see and doesn't want to get dirty. You've changed and are more like your parents, now."

"Those summers at the agency are a big part of that," she explained. "Because of the OGs and Staff Sergeant Royce. They didn't disrespect me, but they also didn't let me get away with being the daughter of James Brownstone. I think of them as family, really. All of them, but particularly Trey and Shorty."

Mason's face tightened. "Shorty's the one who died when your Dad faced the Council."

"Yeah. He died saving Trey. It wasn't like Myna, though. He saved someone he cared about, but it wasn't him trading his life for thousands. I've thought about that often through the years and whether it was a good death." She wound her arms around her knees and pulled them up to her chest. "I don't know what a good death is, Mason. Shorty died destroying an evil magical cabal and saving his best friend. Myna died saving Vancouver from weird monsters. Both of those deaths seem better than the awful way my biological mother died, but they're still deaths. People we care about die and don't come back." She sighed. "Even a wish can't bring the dead back. With all our technology and magic, there's still a firm limit to what we can do."

"The Seventh Order is finished," he declared. "And that's something. There will be far fewer deaths in the future because of it." He inclined his head toward Izzie. "Not only that. Can't you see it?"

"See what?" Alison looked at her friend. The bounty hunter gestured widely and cut through the air with her hand as she explained something to a newly arrived RCMP officer.

"Even though she looks exhausted, there's also freedom there." He sighed. "I used to see that with some of my old clients. They would get a death threat, and the world would weigh on their shoulders. It's hard to live when you always have to worry about someone coming to kill you. The assassin would be caught or killed, and you could actually see that weight lift off the client's shoulders. You could see the knowledge that they had regained control of their life and been freed. We lost someone today, and I won't ever minimize that, but she made the choices all along. The honorable choices. The rational ones." He nodded. "She knew each of those choices might lead to her dying sooner, but she didn't turn away from that because she wanted to make sure her death had some meaning."

"I know all that, but it's still hard." She fixed her gaze on the sky. "Just like it was hard with Shorty and a few of the others who died at the agency throughout the years."

"I've lost friends before," Mason explained. "It's hard to be a bodyguard and not. It's the same thing with you and bounty hunting. We honor their sacrifices and memory." He pulled her into a hug. "And remember, you have people who care about you, A. You don't have to hold the entire weight of the world on your shoulders. And none of this was your fault. You and Izzie didn't start this fight, but you finished it, and you saved a lot of people's lives."

"Thanks," she replied softly. "I needed that."

James broke away from the crowd and headed toward them, frowning. "Is everything okay?"

She smiled. "Yeah, Dad. Mason's helping me take it all in and process things."

He grunted as he stared at the younger man and his eyes narrowed. "You've lost people before? In fights? Not from disease or old age?"

The life wizard nodded. "Yes, Mr. Brownstone. Several times."

Please, Dad. Don't have a big dick contest now. I don't want this.

James looked at each of them before he nodded again, newfound respect in his eyes. "I won't be able to be with her for the aftermath, but you will. I'm depending on you, Mason. A real man doesn't only protect his woman. He also supports her when she has to deal with this kind of shit. Since you're moving in together, that's part of your responsibility." He grunted and walked back toward the crowd he'd chatted with before.

Mason chuckled quietly. "I think that means he officially approves again, and all I had to do was fight by his side in a brutal battle against a fanatical dark wizard order."

"Good. It's one less thing to stress me out." She managed a smile and rested her head on his shoulder. "I just want to sit here and think for a while."

"Take all the time you need, A. I'm never going anywhere."

A couple of hours later, a more relaxed Alison drew away from a conversation with Hana and Lily to head over to Drysi, who stood near the rubble and stared into space. The pain of Myna's death lingered, but there were still the living to consider. Part of being a leader was to attend to those people, no matter how much it hurt.

"Are you okay?" she asked. "You came damned close to dying in there."

The witch chuckled. With the blood and dust all over her, she looked like a deranged psychopath. "I was ready to die, but you saved my ass. I wanted to make sure you destroyed him."

"That we did." She sighed. "But you still didn't answer my question. So, are you okay?"

"Shouldn't I ask you that? I might have almost died, but you lost a friend."

"I'm doing as well as can be expected." She shrugged. "And the Seventh Order is done. I'm sure there are a few operatives out there, but we crushed them completely today. I wouldn't be surprised if no dark wizard gets within a hundred miles of me for a long time." She managed a bitter laugh. "I am a true Brownstone now. I killed an organization, and it ended with their building being destroyed."

"That's true. Right tidy victory this is against those bastards." Drysi shook her head. "I wish I could have been the one to kill him, but the important thing is he's dead. That they're all dead." She licked her lips. "Now, I don't know what I should do. I suppose I'll go back to bounty hunting. I won't have to waste half my time spying on people for the order, so I'll probably make better money at it. It's a good way to clean scum off the streets, and what good is it to be trash if you can't hunt other trash?"

"You're not trash, and there are other options." Alison gestured to Mason in the distance. "We could use another witch with combat experience at the company. You've shown you're good in a fight, and I would be glad to have you back any of us up. I've been worried about finding compatible people who can work with our team, and you can. We haven't even trained together, and you have great instincts. I would have loved a little head's up with that big spell you pulled, but you gave me the opening I needed. Once you work with us more regularly, we'll be unstoppable."

The witch laughed and shook her head as incredulity captured her face. "Are you serious? Alison, I helped you, but that doesn't change what I am. I'm an awful woman who's done awful things. In fact, I'm the kind of woman you would normally kill. I was a willing and knowing member of the Seventh Order. I lied to you from the minute I met you, and I plotted to assassinate you. And you want me to work for you? You actually want to pay me to have your back?"

"Yeah. You'd be surprised how many people I know who have done awful things. This is a difficult world, and the return of magic made things only more challenging." She sighed and nodded at Hana. "When we first met, Hana was about to try to charm me and hand me over to gangsters to pay her debt. Those thugs weren't looking for secretaries. Some of my other friends and even my family have done some nasty things. The past is the past, and the future is the future. I'm not worried about people who show improvement. It's not like I'm a saint, either."

"The past is the past?" Drysi drew her wand and stared at it. "I grew up being taught that my magic marked me as special and made me better than anyone normal. Then, my family told me of the old days and the proud lineage of my dark family, and how we deserved more. I always believed it, and it was easy to take that to the next level and believe only the dark families had any value. I won't lie, I liked the feeling. It felt bloody brilliant to think of myself as a superior being." She shook her head. "No, I didn't only think I was better. I knew I was better, and I had the power to prove it. If I killed a man, I thought that was merely more proof that I deserved to live and he didn't."

Multiple helicopters dotted the sky in the distance.

"And now?" Alison asked softly. "What do you think?"

"Killing people and taking things is something anyone can do. Any street punk can do it." The witch tucked her wand inside her vest. "I deserve to die for the things I've done. I spent all this time convincing myself I was the heir to a noble and proud lineage, but I'm nothing more than a street punk killer with a wand."

The half-Drow shook her head. "There's another way to think about this and another way to think about yourself."

"And what's that?"

She gestured toward the rubble. "You can think about making up for it. You did the right thing when you had a chance. You helped me defeat the order, and you were ready to give your life to do that. If you were merely some petty thug, you would only care about self-preservation, not stopping other bad guys."

Drysi snorted. "That was nothing but petty revenge. I knew I could die happy as long as it ended with that bloody bastard Conrad's death. He was a prick."

"And what about Nereid Island?" she challenged. "You didn't have to risk your life to help them."

"If that storm grew more out of control, I might have died."

Alison shook her head. "And you could have simply let me do it or, for that matter, you could have taken a number of opportunities to kill me. It's not like I walk around with a shield and shadow blade out all the time."

The woman's expression faltered. "I... That was different. And..." She sighed into her hand. "I don't know who I am anymore."

"That's my thing. I always want to give people one last chance." She put her hand on Drysi's shoulder. "I think you've earned it. I can't say that working for me will suddenly wash every bad thing you've ever done away, but a lot of people have already died in this mess with the order. I don't think one more person dying will do much to balance the scales, but helping stop future shit like this? That might, and Brownstone Security does run into a lot of trouble, deserved or otherwise." She took a deep breath and exhaled slowly. "I don't know. Myna spent centuries looking for meaning. I can't promise you that you'll find that with me, but at least you'll be where people will have your back. We won't judge you for your past. We'll only judge you if you don't have our backs."

Her companion stared at a helicopter as it landed a hundred yards away. "Do you really want a witch who used to work for the dark families in your company? You're Alison Brownstone. You're like a…boogeyman to the dark families, and not only the Seventh Order."

Alison smiled. "You're damned right I want you. I want a talented witch in my company, one who helped destroy the Seventh Order." She offered her hand. "But it's like it was with Myna. It's your choice. I could use you, but I also don't want anyone who doesn't want to join us."

Drysi took her hand and gave it a firm shake. "It's a right fair offer, and I accept."

CHAPTER TWENTY-SIX

"Senator Johnston is helping to pull a few strings, but it seems like the Canadian government has tried to downplay the incident, even if they ended up not having a bounty they could use as an excuse." Alison smiled as she set a cup of coffee on her dining room table in front of Izzie. "It looks like everything will turn out all right, but the senator made it clear I should try to not cause any 'major trouble' for a while." She shrugged. "I'll stay out of Canada. Something about Brownstones and Canada always seems to bring trouble."

Her friend chuckled. "The country is far kinder to Berens. I've had a few problems with bounties there, but nothing like the Seventh Order."

"It's not like I run into that kind of thing every week." She laughed. "I don't think I could take it if I did. The average job we have is usually an easy deal. Point A to Point B, or eliminate a threat, but these last few months have been extra crazy."

The bounty hunter nodded and fell silent. She stared

into the dark liquid in front of her. "I almost thought it would never be over. It seems so strange now. I keep thinking it'll start again."

"The fight?" She sighed. "Those monsters?"

Izzie shook her head. "No. Everything. Having to run from the dark wizards and hide. These people have been after me for so long, it's like I took them for granted—like they were some law of nature that came with being alive and not a group of people I could defeat. There was nothing constant in life but death, taxes, and dark wizards hunting my family, and now, it's done. All those years of hiding and living my life like I could die at any second. Now I have a shot at…not being normal, that was never in the cards, but at least having a damned choice. It's sobering to think that I've…that we've won against the dark wizards."

Alison cleared her throat. "Yeah, about that…"

"What? Seventh Order dead-enders?" She frowned. "At this point, I don't care. If they want me, maybe I'll dance naked at the top of the London Eye and wait for them to come to me."

"You'll be able to keep your clothes on." She raised a hand placatingly. "And my news is a good thing. Kind of. I've had a few people contact me in the last few days. Some via my underworld contacts and others using different methods. One person straight-up called me on the phone. All these people are the same, though. They're all representatives of the dark families."

"And?" Izzie's jaw tightened. "What did they have to say? They plan to attack us in force now because we dared to destroy their precious Seventh Order?"

She shook her head. "If anything, it was completely the opposite. They've made it very clear that they disavow the actions of the Seventh Order, and they've pledged to steer clear of both our families. Many of them have made it even more clear that they don't want our negative attention and even went so far as to claim that the Seventh Order were renegades of a sort."

"What bullshit." The bounty hunter snorted. "Plenty of the dark families had no problem helping the Seventh Order when it suited their purposes."

"I'm not saying I believe all that, but I do believe you are no longer a target to them. After all, the main reason they wanted you was to fuel the Great Pillar plan, and that was a Seventh Order mission. I think the dark families are scared. It's a combined Brownstone-Berens Effect." She grinned. "It's fun, isn't it? When the bad guys finally buy a clue, that is."

"So, annihilate an entire elite order of dark wizards, and the rest realize they could be next?" Izzie snickered.

"Yeah, that's the general idea." Alison smiled. "The point is, you're free. You can be with your family or…even…you know, pursue other options."

Her friend shook her head, her expression serious once more. "Like what?"

"We make a great team. We always have." She shrugged. "I'd love to have you at the company."

"I'm sorry, Alison."

"Because of Drysi?"

"Nope. I believe her. Remember, I tested her with a spell. If she falls off the wagon, I know you'll either pull her back or crush her, and it's probably a useful thing to have a woman who knows her way around the dark families in case they ever act up again."

"If it's not Drysi, then what? I thought you would jump at the chance to join the company."

"I don't think I'm ready to settle down like that. It's hard to shift from always being on the run to instantly living in one place. I need to relearn what it's like to not be internationally hunted for a while." Izzie looked thoughtful. "I think I'll stick to bounty hunting for now. At least I can visit you without a bunch of stupid letters and shit."

"Yes, that will be convenient." Alison sighed. "I won't miss not being able to talk to one of my best friends over the phone. Also, you could reach out to Luke. I know I told you before, but he still loves you."

"That's sweet, and a part of my heart will always be with him, but…" A soft smile played across Izzie's face. "It's not a good idea."

"Why not? The only reason you avoided him was to protect him, and he's a grown shifter congressman. He can do a good job of taking care of himself if there's no specific threat."

"You don't understand, Alison." She brought the cup to her mouth and took a sip of coffee. "Which is funny, because you, of all people, should understand."

"Explain it to me."

"Because the girl he fell in love with died a long time ago."

Alison sighed and looked down. "Exactly like with Tanner, even if the circumstances were different."

"Exactly." Izzie put her hand over her heart. "That girl's memories live on in here, but she's gone, replaced by a hard woman who looks back at those memories with fondness but also knows she can't walk back into a life stolen from her." She set her cup down. "I'm not saying I'll never have a relationship, but what I need to do now is look forward, not back. But, even though I won't join the company, thanks for everything, Alison. I couldn't have done this without you. Honestly, you helped me take my life back."

"And I couldn't have done it without you and everyone else. Like I said, we're a great team." She pulled her friend into a hug.

"Yes. A great team."

Alison snuggled into the crook of Mason's arm as they lay in his bed. She was at his house that night after Sonya insisted that she could "survive one night alone by myself."

"Vacation," she declared.

He smiled at her. "What about them?"

"First, all that crap in Japan with Lily and then the Seventh Order and Myna."

He sat up and looked at her. "Are you okay, A?"

"I'm fine. It's… I don't know. I've lost many people in my life, and I didn't know her that long, but I already saw her as someone who would be part of my life." She laid her head on the pillow. "Maybe it's because I never knew my grandparents on either side. Myna was like the cool grandma, except she taught me better spells and how to control my powers."

"I really am sorry." He stroked her hair gently. "I wish there was something I could do."

"You were right before. She made her choice, and she died helping to save people." She sighed. "It'll take me a while to fully adjust to the idea that she's never coming back. It's all too busy. And too much. I want to take a vacation. No concerns about house hunting. No worrying about Drow princesses. We can see if Sonya wants to come along, and if she doesn't—which, let's face it, she probably won't—she can stay with Tahir and Hana for a week and survive." She chuckled. "That reminds me. Did you know that Omni is a bird now?"

"Not a frog anymore?" Mason asked.

Alison shook her head. "Nope, not a frog. They still don't know what triggers the transformations, and their research hasn't turned up what he might be."

"Do you think it's safe for them to have him?"

She shrugged. "Probably not, but Hana will claw the eyes out of anyone who tries to take Omni from her. She loves him. We'll wait until it's a problem and then we'll handle it."

"A vacation? I can see sitting with you in a hammock on some tropical island, you in some sexy little bikini." He grinned.

"Maybe we should go on vacation to Antarctica."

Mason pouted.

She ruffled his hair. "Okay, somewhere tropical."

When an experiment goes awry, a Brownstone is called to the rescue. Alison's adventure continues in <u>A Brownstone Response.</u>

When an experiment goes awry, a Brownstone is called to the rescue. Alison's adventure continues in A Brownstone Response.

AVAILABLE FOR PURCHASE HERE

This fall I turn 60 years old and my goal from here to there is to make peace with everything, find some balance and enter the next decade in style. I don't want to be defined by what 60 is supposed to mean, and instead I want to make up my own definitions. That started with writing the new series, The Peabrain Adventures and it's been a blast. (If you haven't joined in the fun yet – come see what we're up to.)

But, being 59 also means paying it some respect. Back in my twenties I could eat whatever I wanted to, stay up late and fly by the seat of my pants – and with very few consequences. But now, I'm in bed around ten at the latest, which is before the time I would even head out back then.

Older I get, the more I have to do to keep the organic engine running. It's all good. I'm cleaning up my act and actually learning a little more about cooking, yoga, swimming – instead of what bar has the best onion rings. (A quest with an old roommate back in the '80s)

My latest is Ayurveda, which is a lifestyle more than a way of eating that's over a thousand years old from India. I first heard about it 10 years ago when I was first diagnosed with cancer and a few friends sent me some Ayurveda cookbooks. Then it just kept popping up everywhere.

Over time, the way I was eating, which was better, was working less and less and I couldn't figure out why. This lifestyle of eating in balance and according to seasons kept showing up. This past month, I finally decided to dive in and go see a practitioner.

It's only been a week, but I'm surprised at how much better I feel. Mind is clearer, skin looks better, and pants are looser. All good. My goal, in the end is to not enter senior citizenship with a pill box of any size and to be willing to use food as nutrition and medicine instead. I heard Dr. Sanjay Gupta (mentioning Ayurveda again – it was everywhere, like the universe was having a conversation with me) say that in Ayurveda, food is first viewed from a practical stance – what will this do for me – and then from a palate. Side note – the food is delish, and it doesn't cut out anything, it's about balance – when to eat it, how much do you need.

Westerners (that's us) think palate first – how does it taste – and practical second (frankly, if you're at Taco Bell and you're reading this – an old fave place of mine – practical may still be out in the parking lot – let's be real).

So, less than six months to go in my last year of the 50's, and the big new journey has already begun. I want to be ready for what comes next and able to enjoy it to the fullest. That's gonna take being able to get out of the chair without a grunt and waking up without feeling tired. So, Ayurveda me baby!

More adventures to follow.

THANK YOU for not only reading this story but these *Author Notes* as well.

(I think I've been good with always opening with "thank you." If not, I need to edit the other *Author Notes*!)

RANDOM (*sometimes*) THOUGHTS?

Slowing down is a thing. Could be good, might be a bit rough.

I've been reducing my work load and trying to take the bigger part of Sunday's off for the last month.

The good? More books to read to fill in my time.

The bad? Monday morning 'to-do's' piled up from Saturday. It's sometimes bad enough that I stress just looking at all of the notes :-).

So I cheat, just a little. At times, I will look into Slack to see if there are any messages I can answer quickly, or push to Monday. It isn't truly unplugging for the day but my Monday mornings are less stressful and I appreciate being sort of connected.

For three years I built the company daily, and there was only one time (I think) where I didn't do anything business related, and most days were 8-14 hours.

A 'two' hour day was a vacation.

Now, I'm dealing with stepping back and it's going ok. I think I will survive and the company (I suspect) might be a little bit better for it.

AROUND THE WORLD IN 80 DAYS

One of the interesting (at least to me) aspects of my life is the ability to work from anywhere and at any time. In the future, I hope to re-read my own *Author Notes* and remember my life as a diary entry.

Cave in the Sky (™) Las Vegas, Nv - USA

A few CC's today with different people, discussed green-lighting a project with JL Hendricks having to do with a Fae Academy series - working on my Opus X project and answered multiple questions around the company.

Then, my son called.

He's doing something drastic in his life (moving states) and there isn't much to say. He's going to do it, and all we can do as his parents is fret.

No one told me about the fretting part when I was having kids. For whatever reason, my mind didn't think about them causing me so much anxiety AFTER they were out of the house.

It's times like this I wished I drank ;-)

Actually, I don't. But if you don't have your humor - what else do you have?

FAN PRICING

$0.99 Saturdays (new LMBPN stuff) and $0.99 Wednesday (both LMBPN books and friends of LMBPN books.) Get great stuff from us and others at tantalizing prices.

Go ahead, I bet you can't read just one.

Sign up here: http://lmbpn.com/email/.

HOW TO MARKET FOR BOOKS YOU LOVE

Review them so others have your thoughts, tell friends and the dogs of your enemies (because who wants to talk with enemies?)... *Enough said ;-)*

Ad Aeternitatem,

Michael Anderle

www.ingramcontent.com/pod-product-compliance
Lightning Source LLC
Chambersburg PA
CBHW050239110726
47898CB00007B/2209